P9-DFX-223

He climbed into the car as the train pulled out of the siding. Charley Colt saw him and stepped backward slowly, steeled to the task at hand.

"What? Ain't scared all of a sudden?" he growled

"Why should I be?" Charley grinned. "I'm the one with the gun on my hip."

He took a menacing step forward and said, "You ain't gonna.shoot an innocent man in cold blood. If you kill me it's *murder*."

Charley drew and fired. The bullet caught him in the stomach and knocked him back two steps. His eyes opened wide as Charley holstered the .44, walked up to him, and said, "It's also *justice*."

A swift kick to the chest sent him backward off the train and into the night air.

Ten cars back, Chris Colt and Man Killer saw the man's body falling to the ground. They also saw Charley ducking back inside. "That little guy is killing off Meconi's gang!" Colt exclaimed.

"That is not all," Man Killer said. "That little guy is your sister."

MATCHED COLTS

EAGLE
by Don Bendell

Chris Colt didn't believe in the legendary Sasquatch, no matter if witnesses told of a monstrously huge figure who slew victims with hideous strength and vanished like smoke in the air. But now in the wild Sangre de Cristo mountains of Colorado, even Chris Colt, the famed Chief of Scouts, felt a tremor of unease in his trigger finger. The horrifying murderer he was hunting was more brutal than any beast he had ever heard of, and more brilliant than any man he had ever had to best. Colt was facing the ultimate test of his own strength, skill, and savvy against an almost inhuman creature whose lethal lust had turned the vast unspoiled wilderness into an endless killing field. A creature who called himself—Eagle. . . .

from SIGNET

Ed

MATCHED COLTS

Don Bendell

A SIGNET BOOK

SIGNET
Published by the Penguin Group
Penguin Books USA Inc., 375 Hudson Street,
New York, New York 10014, U.S.A.
Penguin Books Ltd, 27 Wrights Lane,
London W8 5TZ, England
Penguin Books Australia Ltd,
Ringwood, Victoria, Australia
Penguin Books Canada Ltd, 10 Alcorn Avenue,
Toronto, Ontario, Canada M4V 3B2
Penguin Books (N.Z.) Ltd, 182-190 Wairau Road,
Auckland 10, New Zealand

Penguin Books Ltd, Registered Offices:
Harmondsworth, Middlesex, England

First published by Signet, an imprint of Dutton Signet,
a division of Penguin Books USA Inc.

First Printing, April, 1997
10 9 8 7 6 5 4 3 2 1

DEDICATION

Heed my words for they are of iron. I speak now of my brother, my fellow warrior, and great warrior-chief who I admire. We have sometimes fought side by side in great battles, and we have treated each other's wounds. He has gone into battle many times, this strongheart, and he has counted many first coups; yet this brave likes to grow and smell flowers. He likes to read the big book of the Wasicun, which tells of the Great Mystery, His Son, and of great Love. He also smokes the sacred pipe and makes careful and wise decisions. He listens to the young elks bugle and thrash the trees about him, but he just smiles instead of hooking them on his mighty antlers. For almost fifty summers, my winter count has grown much longer with many pictures on it, and for more than half, he has been there. This book is dedicated to you mighty warrior, wise chief, and great friend Master Bob Chaney.

In God's love,

Don Bendell

ACKNOWLEDGMENTS

I would, once again, like to thank Director Gary Shook and the staff of the Canon City District Library, especially the Local Archives, for their assistance in the research about the southern Colorado area. I would also like to thank my longtime close friend and karate instructor, who this book is dedicated to, Master Bob Chaney for your friendship and fine example of being a tough-minded and very spiritual warrior, who uses his head and common sense instead of choosing battle, and who is so effective in teaching others the same attitude.

Finally, I would like to thank my friend, Colorado State Attorney General Gale Norton, my wife, Shirley, and women like them who are paving the way for other women to follow. I thank them for teaching us all that sometimes "the best man for the job is a woman."

Eagle's Mate

And so she flew from tree to tree
Collecting sticks wher'er she flew,
The eagle's mate who shares my nest,
With heart and mind of gold.

She flies to far-off dizzy heights
And brings back food to feed the nest
And climbs on stormy angry winds
To search for food or twigs or such.

She builds the aerie tight with wood
And watches over those who follow.
I ofttimes worry about her work
So frenzied, hard, and hours-long.

But then, but then I know this isn't so,
Least not with eagles, anyhow.
For, it's the struggle and the work
That gives us sinewed, spreading wings.

So now I watch my eagle's mate
Riding upslopes cross the range
Hunting snowshoes or nesting tools
While watching far horizons.

I love you, Shirley,

Don Bendell

"A Lady with a Lamp shall stand
In the great history of the land,
A noble type of good,
Heroic womanhood."

From *Santa Filomena*

by Henry Wadsworth Longfellow

CHAPTER 1

Daddy

Even as a teenaged girl, Charlotte Baldwin was a beautiful young woman who looked much older than her years. She knew that she must look good because of so many comments from the boys at school and church. In fact, for the past year, a number of the men in town made her feel uncomfortable by the way they looked at her or the comments they made. Her hair looked as if it had been dipped into a vat of honey, and it was slowly dripping from the ends of it in the bright summer sun. Her eyes were a very deep dark blue and were above a pair of high cheekbones, and there was a great deal of intelligence show-ing in those eyes. Her body was full and filled and bulged the material of anything she wore. Her choice had usually been to wear homespun trousers and flannel shirts, while she went out tracking or hunting whitetail deer or javelina, wild pigs in the thickets around her family's south Texas home, patterned after her father's plantation that burned down in Georgia during the Civil War. She was an absolute tomboy and could out hunt, fish, or track any of the boys around, but the reason she liked those things was because so many males carried on about her beauty from the time she could remember. Charley wanted to be appreciated for what she could do and what she thought about, not the way she looked.

Their home did not look anything like the Mexican-influenced architecture of south Texas in the 1870s. It seemed as if it had been transplanted from their native South Carolina. The main house had large white columns and a veranda that wrapped all the way around the bottom floor. With the finished attic, it stood three stories tall, but the ceilings on each floor were very high. There was a long turnaround driveway that curved right in front of the main double doors.

The stables were also whitewashed with topline thoroughbreds in stall after stall. There were two long stable buildings, plus a large whitewashed hay barn, with an attached grain silo and indoor lunging and training arena. Behind the stables were several small shacks that looked to be sharecropper quarters. Descendants of former slaves lived in those cramped buildings.

King's Ransom was a beautiful chestnut stallion with a white blaze and four white stockings. He was the other pastime for Charley Baldwin. If she wasn't hunting or fishing, she was either riding or grooming him.

It was a hot night in August of her sixteenth year that Charlotte paid one of her nightly visits to the big horse. Her mother had been thrown jumping a large gray gelding and her neck was broken and there seemed to be internal injuries that the doctor could do nothing about. Her mother had been coughing up blood and once it started running out of her ears. Her father, Adam Baldwin, had been drinking heavier than usual and was in one of his foul moods.

Charlotte forked some fresh bedding straw into King's stall and then brought him an apple from the barrel in the corner. Being careful not to bend her fingers around the little red fruit, so they wouldn't get bitten, she held the apple out on her flat palm.

The horse sniffed the apple, then pulled his lips back as if he were smiling and bit down on it, crunching it in two. He chewed it slowly while Charley held the other half up for him to eat at his leisure. King pulled the other part into his mouth using his wrinkled lips then slowly chewed it, the bites making a slight echo within the confines of his large mouth and the wooden stall.

Nightgown blowing out with the breeze, Charlotte smiled and turned to go back to the house. She stopped dead in her tracks and a serious look fell over her beautiful countenance.

"Charley, my darling," her father said, weaving in his stance near the hay pile, "Ah'm afraid, Mother will not be with us much longer. We just have each other now."

He took a step forward and Charlotte's eyes searched the stables for a weapon. She spotted the pitchfork and held it in front of her menacingly. Tears flooded her eyes, as he again called her by the nickname her mother had given her so many years before.

"Charley, now Ah am your father, sweetheart," Adam slurred, "we must keep our secret and always be close. That's how a family that loves each other is. Set the fork down, girl."

"No, Daddy, we aren't going to have any secrets," Charlotte said. "You will keep your hands off of me, or I swear by all that is holy, I'll stick you like I was hunting for frog legs. Understand?"

He sat down and put his face in his hands and started sobbing uncontrollably.

Between sobs, he mumbled, "Mama's going to die."

Charlotte started crying, too, and she set the fork down and started toward him, but hesitated. She wanted desperately to put her hands around him and hold him tight, but she dare not. Her hand went forward hesitatingly to touch his hair, but she paused.

Suddenly, his right hand shot out and grabbed her by the wrist, yanking her into his arms. He tried to kiss her while she kicked and screamed.

Adam said, "Now, Charlotte. Ah am your father and you shall do as I say, young lady. Ah just want to show you how much I love you."

She calmed down and steeled herself to the task before her. She relaxed and seemed to submit, and he tilted her head up to kiss her.

Charlotte suddenly brought her right knee up as hard as she could into his groin. The air left him in a rush. He clutched himself with both hands and made an unusual whining sound. He reached for her with his right hand and grabbed her nightgown, which tore away, but she swung a kick viciously at his kneecap. It missed but almost collapsed his left leg as it struck him on the thigh just above the kneecap. He howled in pain and grabbed it as she started to run again.

He cornered her and she fought back as he held her with both hands.

"Let go!" she screamed.

She stomped on his foot, and he released one hand. Charley swung a right hook that caught him on the edge of the jaw and he spun falling face-first into a large pile of horse manure. He stood with a yell and was brought up short by the voice of Corrie the housekeeper.

Corrie said, "Missy Charley, Missus Baldwin wants ta see ya right away."

Charlotte nodded gratefully and ran past Corrie, tears flooding her eyes. Adam started after her but Corrie stepped directly in his path. She had pulled an apple out of the barrel and now started peeling it with a large knife she had in the folds of her apron. Corrie was a large woman whose parents had been captured by slave traders in southern Africa and were sold at auction to Adam's father.

Corrie stared into his eyes while she peeled the

apple slowly. There was no play in her eyes right now.

Corrie said, "Mastah Baldwin, mah mama and my papa was slaves fo yo papa, an kept on wif him after de war. I has worked fo yo family all mah life, too. But, I wants ta tell you somthin', suh, and makes sure yo unnerstand. If you evah tech thet girl again, Ah'll run ya through with a dull blade ovah and ovah agin, suh. We unnerstand each othah?"

He nodded his head meekly and fell on his rear end into the hay pile, a blank look on his reddened face. Corrie turned and left.

Charlotte hesitated before going into her mother's room. It was always a place of wonder and safety when she was growing up. She loved to climb into bed with Mommy when her father wasn't around. She felt safe with her, but soon her mother would be dead. She hated facing it, but she could tell, and her mother had always taught her to face up to anything, good or bad.

She brushed her hair back and smiled, then opened the door and swept into the room. Her face did not belie her true feelings, for when she saw her beloved mother it almost broke her heart. The beautiful woman had been lingering near death and had been holding on just to speak with Charlotte. It showed. She weakly patted the bed beside her and smiled with effort. Charlotte went over and sat down. Corrie entered the room and sat down on the bed by Charlotte.

Mrs. Baldwin said, "Charley, I asked Corrie to come here, too, darling, for I want you to hear what I have to say. Corrie, reach into my nightstand here and bring out the small bag in there, please?"

Corrie smiled, tears in her eyes, and complied. She pulled out a handbag with embroidery on it.

Mrs. Baldwin said, "Now, I am a dying woman."

Charlotte started to interrupt but the mother held up her finger.

Mrs. Baldwin said, "Do not interrupt or argue. I know I am dying, and you shall have to accept it. I am making a dying request. Open the bag, Corrie."

Corrie did so and her eyes opened wide as she saw the money inside. It had to be thousands of dollars. She closed the bag and looked at her benefactor.

Mrs. Baldwin went on, "You have served our family well and faithfully, and my husband is a scoundrel. After the funeral, take that money and your family and leave. Go make a life for your-self somewhere. You deserve it, Corrie."

Corrie started sobbing uncontrollably, as she fell forward and held Mrs. Baldwin carefully by the shoulders. The dying woman stroked her hair.

Mrs. Baldwin said, "Come on, brave up. You have to be of a keen mind, Corrie."

She then looked at her daughter and tears came into her own eyes as she said, "Charley, Adam Baldwin is not your real father."

Charlotte looked shocked and glanced at Corrie who also looked shocked.

Mrs. Baldwin, smiling, explained, "There was a shoemaker from Cuyahoga Falls, Ohio, who I met when I went north to visit my Yankee cousins in Akron, Ohio. There was a beautiful place in the woods, along the Cuyahoga River between Akron and Cuyahoga Falls, which I vis-ited with my cousins. There was a large area cut out of the rock maybe sixty feet high and at least as wide. They say the Indians used to meet and powwow in there. I left the place one day, with my cousins, but told them I wanted to return by myself, while they fished upstream in the river.

"When I came upon the cavern, I heard sob-bing, and from a deep voice, so I approached slowly and carefully. I saw this man, a tall hand-some one he was, and he had cast himself across a rock and was crying."

Charlotte still had a look of shock on her face.

Charlotte's mother went on, "I called out to him, and he jumped up, drying his eyes and smiling but quite embarrassed. He explained that he had lost his wife, and this was a place where they used to come when they were court-ing. He had a young son named Christopher. We saw each other for several weeks, while I visited and we fell deeply in love with each other. My family made me leave to return back south, but you were already conceived by that time, the re-sult of our deep love for each other. Adam Bald-win had been after my father to get me to marry him, for his family had plenty of money as you well know. He has basically spent or lost most of it ever since he inherited it."

Charlotte said, "Whatever became of the man, Mother?"

Mrs. Baldwin said, "My parents told me he had been killed in a gun battle, and it broke my heart, so I didn't resist when they forced me to marry Adam. Later, I found out that he didn't die, but when he learned of my marriage, he did start drinking heavily and was stabbed in a bar fight in Ohio. He lingered for a short while but did die eventually."

"What was his name, Mother?" Charlotte asked, not really knowing what else to say.

Mrs. Baldwin said, "I have an envelope for you in the drawer explaining about him and what I know. His last name was Colt, and I shall soon be joining him in heaven, dear, and I couldn't be happier. That money is your escape money if you ever have to leave. I know how rough it has been for you with that scoundrel, dear, but I have taught you to be a survivor, and you shall. Just promise me one thing?"

Charlotte said, "Anything, Mother. I love you with all my heart."

Weakly, the mother responded, "And I, you, sweetheart. Promise me that no matter what, you will only marry for love. Please tell me that, and I can leave happy."

Tears in her eyes, Charlotte said, "I swear it, Mother. I swear it by all that is holy. I will only marry for love."

Mrs. Baldwin smiled with genuine happiness.

Downstairs, on the veranda, two big tough-looking cowboys were speaking with Adam Baldwin. He offered them a drink and a butler brought the three of them snifters of brandy.

The taller one swallowed his in one gulp, set the glass down, and punched Baldwin in the stomach. The paunchy man started vomiting and clutched at his abdomen, trying to keep from choking on brandy and vomit.

The tall one said, "Baldwin, this shore is a nice spread ya got hyar. Hate ta see it burn to the ground, but ya got one more week, or it will. Ya pay yer gamblin' debts in Texas, Mister, or ya pay in blood. Fact, thet shore is one purty little gal ya got. Maybe it'll be her blood gettin' spilt."

The funeral was attended by many people near and far. There wasn't a dry eye at the graveside, as Mrs. Baldwin was laid to rest.

It was the night of the funeral and Charlotte lay in her bed crying. Her mother was gone and Corrie and her family left right after the funeral. It had been a tearful good-bye, but Charlotte was happy for Corrie, who she referred to as Aunt Corrie. The woman had to take care of her children, and Charlotte knew that they would be miserable around Adam Baldwin.

There was a flash of lightning outside and Charley hunched her shoulders waiting for the clap of thunder. It started as a rumble and suddenly there was a loud crash as her door flew open and Adam Baldwin staggered into the room. He had a bottle of brandy in his right hand, and a very mean look in his eyes.

Charlotte jumped out of bed, slamming her back against the wall as her father half dived, half fell onto the feather mattress. Whimpering, she ran past him and out the door, before he could recover and grab her.

Out in the hallway, Charlotte stopped and turned at the door. She left her clothes and the envelope her mother gave her. More importantly, she left the cameo her mother left her, as well.

Charlotte gritted her teeth, grabbed the knob, turned it, and entered her bedroom. Adam stood in front of her, five feet away, an evil grin on his unshaven face.

"Sho," he said, "ya finally came to yer senses, Charley. I'm yore daddy, and . . ."

Charlotte interrupted angrily, "No, you're not. My real daddy would have killed you for what you've tried with me."

He gritted his teeth now and took two steps forward, only to be met by a vicious punch to the point of his jaw. Adam staggered back and fell over a footstool, tripping backward and striking his head on the night table. He lay there snoring.

Charlotte ran to the closet and threw on a flannel shirt, a pair of denims, and some boots. She grabbed the envelope with the large bills and the letter and cameo from her mother and tucked them away inside her blouse. She was angry and would not stay under the same roof with this man again.

Adam staggered to his feet and blocked the door from the big walk-in closet. He rubbed his jaw and didn't seem to notice or remember why it hurt.

There was a chuckle and a flaming torch flew behind him, settling against the far wall at the base of the curtains, which caught immediately. Charlotte and Adam both looked and the tall cowboy stood there, gun in hand.

The cowboy smiled at Adam and said, "I warned ya, Baldwin."

He squeezed the trigger, and the gun boomed loud in the room amid the crackle of the spreading flames. Adam flew into the louvered doors, splintering them and staining the doors with crimson. Charlotte screamed as she saw her stepfather slide to the floor.

The cowboy said, "Girlie, ya kin jest put on one a them nightgowns. Make things easier fer me an mah pards. Let's hurry."

Charlotte walked forward and smiled at the

man. She reached up and started to unbutton the top button on her blouse.

She said, "That was my stepfather and I hated him. You want to help me change, sir?"

He licked his lips and reached out.

Her right hand lashed out and he screamed as he dropped the pistol and grabbed his wrist. The cowboy saw the coat hanger in her hand, but too late. She swung it back and lashed it across his face, then swung again and cut the bridge of his nose open.

Charley bent down and grabbed the man's pistol as she pulled out a knife. He took one step forward, and she fired, then fired again, and again. Three bullets in his chest, he staggered backward and fell over the banister to the foyer below.

Charlotte heard voices. "That's Zeke!"

Another said, "Come on, boys!"

She kept her cool. She had to.

Outside the window was a large cottonwood tree. The full branches were several feet from the house, and Adam had complained several times that they were growing too close to Charley's bedroom window. He told her mother that he was worried that some young lad could sneak in her window at night. The mother, however, suspected that he felt that out of jealousy. She had seen the way he had been looking at her daughter.

The curtains, window frame, wall, and even the ceiling were now in flames around the window. Charlotte was very muscular and had always been athletic. She had a major decision to make. She heard shouts and footsteps coming up the winding stairway, and her decision was made.

Charlotte grabbed her pillow off her bed and held it in front of her. She ran across her bedroom, pressed the pillow against her face, and dived head-first through the light-framed window with a crash and tinkling of broken glass. Charley immediately let go of the pillow and stretched her arms out in front of her. She felt herself crashing into branches and twigs and her right, then left, hands hit a thick branch and grabbed it.

Her legs swung up under her, and her belly hit a stump of a thick branch, and it knocked the wind out of her. She wanted to let go, but Charley had a hardheaded quality about her that kept her from quitting once her mind was set to a course of action. Knowing that shots would soon follow her, she looked down, saw another large branch, and dropped. Her left shin scraped against the branch trunk and she cried out, but she grabbed hold of that branch and found herself now hanging only ten feet above the ground.

Charlotte dropped and landed on the balls of her feet, somersaulted forward, just as a shot hit the ground behind her, and she sprinted toward the barn. The whole house was now quickly sprouting flames.

Charlotte made it to the stables with no more bullets coming near her, because of all the large cottonwoods in the yard. She released the horses from their stalls, as she knew that these men would probably set the stables and outbuildings ablaze, as well.

She grabbed a bridle off a peg and ran to the stall of King's Ransom. She heard voices again and Charley didn't worry about a saddle. She put the bridle on and saw one of the cowboys dashing across the yard toward her. Charlotte didn't have time. A voice of a man running along the front of the stables startled her. Charley grabbed a handful of mane and swung up on the back of her beloved chestnut. The big red horse seemed to sense the urgency of the situation and when she hit her heels to his ribs, he bolted as if he had been shot out of a cannon. She gripped his sides with her legs wrapped as tight as she could squeeze, as the seventeen-hands-tall horse jumped over the Dutch door of the stall just as one of the cowboys, gun drawn, appeared in the doorway. The horse's front hooves hit the man in the face, killing him instantly.

The horse corrected with its front feet but still stumbled when he landed and almost went on his nose. Although her momentum pushed her forward over his neck, Charley pulled straight up on the reins, and it helped him correct his balance. The horse took off across the yard weaving in and out of trees, as Charley leaned forward over the neck of the animal. Bullets whizzed all around her, and she heard shouts behind her as the cowboys headed for their own horses.

After a mile, Charlotte slowed her stallion to a fast trot, not worrying about the cowboys catching her in a long chase on their quarter horses. Running across a corral or up a steep hillside, she would be worried, but not on a long race. She was on a thoroughbred, and raising horses, Charley knew as much as anyone else about them.

She knew that the men would come after her, so she headed for the big oak thickets about ten miles from her home. Charlotte lived in Texas, not New York, and there was not a town for her to ride into and report to the constables.

She would have to outwit these men and then go for help. The best place for her to get away from them would be the woods and thickets that she knew. She had become quite a tracker and hunter, and the thicket where she headed was large, had several water holes, and was where she hunted whitetails and javelina.

Charlotte made it there in one hour. About one-quarter of a mile into the thicket there was a jumble of boulders, and she entered these, and kept riding all around and through them. The boulders were surrounded by stands of scrub oaks and some cedars. She rode right through the pathways and straight into the little thickets. It would take the men a long time to unravel her trail, and if they were smart, they would just slowly circle the general area until they found her tracks leading away. Fortunately, Charley thought, these men did not seem to be too intelligent.

She went deep into the thicket to an area she knew that was a clearing with a brook that flowed through it, and it was surrounded by numerous dead saplings from a twister that had set down there when she was a young girl. Although the tornado had stripped and blown away many of the twigs and leaves from the trees, it had also twisted numerous trees into grotesque shapes and left large branches strewn everywhere. They had all, of course, died and became very dry.

Two years later, a lightning bolt had started a fire in the midst of all this and burned the very center of the area where the cyclone had touched down, but the rain with the storm quickly put out the fire. In the years since, the area in the center had grown green with tall lush grasses, kept healthy by a combination of sunshine and the water from the creek.

Although there was no cover, it made an ideal hideout, because nobody could move without making noise through the area of broken, dry branches, saplings, and blown-down, full-size trees. For this reason, it had also been her favorite hunting spot for big whitetails. The big bucks would go into the meadow, bed down, water, and were gone whenever anything entered the area, because they either smelled or heard them long before they came into sight. She had learned to sneak up on some of those big bucks, too, by using stealth and care. She learned elementary things the hard way, such as not step-

ping over logs because of rattlesnakes underneath. She was almost bitten twice.

She also learned, just by spooking enough animals, that whitetail deer could not see off to the
side when they were grazing. If the wind was
right, she learned she could almost sneak up to
them, if she watched their trails when they
grazed. When the deer was about to raise his
head, a nerve in his tail would make the tail
twitch ever so slightly. This was her signal to
freeze in place and somehow the deer did not see
her when she froze. She was not aware that bio-
logically the rods in the deer's type of eyesight
precluded them from seeing her if she was sta-
tionary and that they could not see her when
their head was down grazing. She just discovered this on her own by trial and error and did
not question why. It had provided much meat for
her family and Aunt Corrie's family, as well.

Now, in her favorite hunting grounds she
would make herself a lean-to and cook over a
smokeless fire. She had an abundance of dry
wood to draw from. King would have plenty of
water and graze, although he always had been
grained, hayed, and pampered. She believed it
would be good for him, for she had always been

pampered, too, but was not really afraid of fending on her own in the woods.

Charlotte was now grateful for her abusive stepfather, because wanting to always stay away from him had actually forced her to enjoy a life that would now save her, maybe.

The first thing she did was to take the bridle off her horse and let him start grazing and water. She felt that he would stay there, because there was little graze among the surrounding fields of dry wood, and it was not an area a horse would feel comfortable walking through.

Next, she ran back to the area where they entered the blowdowns and started wiping away the trail as best she could. It would be past dark before she could get back to her campsite, but it was very important to cover the trail now.

She returned to the camp right at dark, satisfied that she had satisfactorily covered her trail. Under the light of a full moon, Charlotte gathered up a good supply of firewood. Then she used branches to fashion a large lean-to frame. Next, she interwove evergreen and cottonwood branches through the frame to give her shelter. Unfortunately, though, Charlotte did not know how to start a fire without matches, she had no food, no weapons, and no warm clothing to ward off the cold.

Charley lay down by the piles of tinder and firewood. Tomorrow, she decided, she would figure it all out, but for now, she had to finally face the events of the day, especially her mother's funeral. Charlotte started crying and then the floodgates burst open. She sobbed openly and then wailed. Maybe the killers would hear her, but she could not help herself. There was too much pain, too much sorrow. She cried so much that she worried about getting sick, and she was totally exhausted. Charley didn't remember falling asleep.

Charlotte was sitting on a branch in the top of a tree with her back against the trunk. She was napping and a noise brought her wide awake. Around her was an entire forest of dead full trees, all hardwoods. There was not a leaf anywhere. The noise that had awakened her was loud, and it happened again.

She looked at someone coming at her across the top of the branches. It was her stepfather. She cried and tried to scream but couldn't. The words wouldn't come out of her mouth. She kept straining, but she just could not get the scream out. It was frustrating and very frightening.

Charley's eyes opened wide, and she sat straight up panting hard, her racking breaths trying to split her open at the seams. She looked around and wiped spittle off her cheek. Charlotte looked from side to side and suddenly realized that she was now really very wide awake. She also knew that something was wrong. She shook her head to clear the cobwebs and then stretched and yawned.

She heard a stick crack in the distance and immediately understood what was happening. The killers were after her and were closing in on her hideout. Charlotte was wide awake now and quickly jumped to her feet. She kicked the firewood pile apart and hoped that her lean-to would just look like a bush if seen from a distance.

She grabbed the bridle and clucked to King. The horse raised his head and looked toward her. He whinnied once, then put his head back down and continued grazing. She walked toward him and the big chestnut continued to graze until she was a few feet away. He stepped forward and grazed some more, head still down. Charley was frustrated. This kept on for a full minute, with him walking slowly forward, hand outstretched.

Charley was so frustrated and scared that she

actually laughed at the situation, whispering, "Of all the times for you to act like a stupid horse, King."

Charlotte picked up several stones off the ground and rubbed them together in her hands, trying to simulate the sound of grain in a bucket. It was enough to make the big horse raise his head and stand still while she approached. He cautiously sniffed toward her hand and she slowly slipped the bridle over his neck. He started to lift his head in defiance, but King was curious enough to find out if she had corn or oats in her hand. Holding the reins around his neck so he wouldn't take off again, she slipped the bit into his mouth and slid the bridle up over his head, carefully tucking the ears under the poll band. She fastened the left side of the cheek band and reached under his neck, throwing the right rein up over his neck. Then she grabbed it and the left rein in her left hand, grabbed a handful of mane with her right, and swung her right leg up and over his back, as she jumped off the left leg. She had to pull a little on the neck, but made it up over the back of the large horse.

She squeezed her calves against his rib cage and said, "Walk."

The horse carefully picked his way through

the morass of broken branches and tree trunks, as he rode away from the approaching riders.

Just before Charlotte left the blowdown area and entered the dense hardwood thicket, she spotted the front killer looking at her tracks on the ground and leading a big gray horse. They were weaving through the jumble of dead tree parts and making steady progress.

She made it into the trees without being spotted and watched for a while from the shadows. The other two killers appeared behind the tracker but spread apart a little from each other. Both of them were mounted.

Charlotte's mind raced. She had to think of something, and she was not expert enough and hadn't the time to effectively cover her trail. She kept riding and thinking but was sensible enough not to try to ride quickly. The last thing she needed was to run her head into a low-hanging branch or break her horse's leg stepping in a hole.

Finally, Charlotte stopped her horse and dismounted. She tied his reins to a low branch sticking out from a sapling, and she looked around the ground for a weapon. She selected a long thick stick and hid with it next to a large oak near the sapling where King was tied.

She waited. Thirty minutes passed and the tracker showed up riding the big gray horse. His eyes were on the ground, until he looked up and spotted King, just twenty steps away. She carefully peered around the tree and could not see the other riders approaching yet. Charley was more frightened than at any time in her life. She knew though that these men would stay after her, so she steeled herself to the task at hand. She needed a weapon, food, and matches.

The man dismounted and walked slowly toward the red horse, gun drawn. He looked all around and kept turning his head toward the rear. He made it to the horse and looked back quickly. Nothing was there. He turned his head and saw a big stick swinging at his face.

He ducked as quickly as he could out of reflex and the stick tore his cheek open as it swished by, slightly bruising the cheekbone as well. The tracker, Bond Cardy, swore and screamed at the same time, but he didn't fall down dead like Charley had hoped. Instead, he lunged forward with a rage, blocking a second swing with the stick and grabbed her roughly by the wrists.

He threw her down on the ground and said, through clenched teeth, "You marked me, girl, so ah'm a gonna mark you fer life, my own way."

She screamed. "No!" as he knelt down, a satanic look in his eyes.

Charlotte's mind raced as she heard a voice yell out, "Bond, where are ya?"

The attacker responded, "Over heah. C'mon, boys, we're gonna have some fun!"

There was no more time to be wasted. Charley's hand shot up and grabbed the front of Bond's homespun brown trousers right at the groin. Her fingers grabbed firm hold of the soft tissue, and she squeezed and twisted with all of her might.

The attacker screamed out in pain, and she grabbed his pistol hand and squeezed his fingers against the hard steel and made him scream in even more pain. She let go of his crotch and grabbed the gun with both hands, twisting it from his hand. Charlotte brought the gun up and back down in a vicious arc, smashing his other cheekbone and knocking him out cold in the process.

"Wal, wall, wal. Ain't she a tough little she-cat, Tuff?"

"I should say, Ab, that she is."

The voices snapped her head around, and she saw the other two killers stepping out of the trees leading their horses and holding rifles in their hands.

She was soon tied, standing with arms and legs outstretched between two trees.

Charley was even more scared as the others splashed water on the face of Bond. He got up rubbing his jaw and shaking his head. He moved forward, upon seeing the beautiful young captive, a look of silent fury chiseled on his bearded face. Charlotte tried to hide her fear as he approached her, and suddenly, he lashed out and backhanded her across the face. Her head snapped to the left, and she tasted blood, as her lower lip split open.

Now, her fear was gone. The anger took over and this was followed by her extremely strong survival instinct.

Ab, a short, wiry gun-tough, said, "Now, Bond, we don't blame ya none fer bein' upset, but don' go spoilin' the merchandise."

Bond pouted, "Did ya see what she done ta me?"

Tuff, a large bearded redhead, wearing dark glasses from failing eyesight due to syphilis, said, "What you talkin' about, spoilin' the merchandise, Abner?"

Ab said, "Wal, take a look at the purty little

thing. We're gonna kill her anyhow. She ain'ta gonna talk."

Bond agreed, "Yeah, nobody'll ever know what happens to her. She's gonna be dead anyhows."

Tuff said, "I don't care. This ain't New York City or New Orleans. This is the West. I run with a gang of the roughest hombres you ever seen, three year back. We had us some boys thet would plug a banker if he looked cross-eyed during a holdup. Wal, one night, after a big bank job, we all went into Cheyenne ta celebrate and had us a good bit a red-eye. One of the boys decides ta molest a Chinee laundry gal. That ol' boy died a hemp fever, buds. We stretched his neck from a stout old cottonwood not far south a Cheyenne. I ain't a party ta molestin' women, son. This is the frontier, they ain't enough of them out here to start thet mess."

Bond fumed, "Didja' see how she's marked me, Tuff? She's marked me permanent."

Charlotte had heard enough. She had a temper and sometimes it just blew.

She said flatly, "You dastardly varmints. If you think you're going to touch one hair on my head without the fight of your life, then your brains are in your boots. I'll cut off two fingers of any man for any time I am touched inappropriately."

Ab said, "What the hell d'she say?"

Bond said, "Don't pay no never mind. She's jest a woman."

Defiant, he walked over to her and grabbed her left breast, saying, "My fingers are all there."

She spit in his face and said, "Cut me loose, you cowardly cur, and they won't be. You just decided to lose ten fingers all at once, Mister."

Bond's temper flared again as he wiped the spit but then laughed as he grabbed her other breast, saying, "Mah fingers are all still here, and Ah shore am glad."

She said defiantly, "Now you'll lose that whole arm."

Ab laughed at this remark, and even Tuff joined in.

She stared at Tuff and said, "Real man of the West, aren't you. How did you get the name Tuff? From raping and killing young women?"

He couldn't stand that and walked over to her pulling out a large Bowie knife, while his friends stared in wonder.

She wanted to scream but couldn't even swallow. He reached out with the knife, blade up, and cut through her bonds. His two cohorts cursed, and she rubbed her wrists, then her ankles.

He turned to his partners and said, "Efn' ya two want ta have her, I ain't gonna interfere, but at least she gits an even break."

He thought that would clear his conscience a little as he walked away from her, head down, but it didn't.

Both of the other men laughed evilly as they approached her.

Ab said, "Fair 'nuff, Tuff. She ain't but a drop of water."

Bond, rubbing his nose, though, held back a little as they both approached her. Ab got a few feet away and wondered how he should grab her safely. She suddenly spit in his eyes, and he immediately and unconsciously wiped his face. That was the opportunity she had planned for and went into his chest head-first, as her right hand grabbed for the gun in his holster. The next thing she knew, it was out and cocked and pointing at Bond, who tried to rush her. He stopped dead in his tracks and threw his hands up. Ab looked up, still holding his bruised breastbone and felt suddenly weak in the knees.

Tuff, near the campfire, reached for a Winchester carbine but stopped at Charley's words, "Go ahead. My last name's Colt, and the colonel was my uncle. Want to find out how equal he made people?"

He stood up and raised his hands.

"No, ma'am," Tuff said, "you made a believer outta me, and I deserve a bullet anyhows. Ah'm so ashamed a myself."

She was confused, frightened, and angry, but she knew she had to either kill all three men or take a very strong stand right now.

She said, "Go ahead, Tuff. Pick up that rifle with your fingers and carry it to me by the end of the barrel."

He complied.

She said, "Now, your knife."

Again, ashamed and hanging his head, he complied.

She then directed him to tie Bond to the tree and to bring her their saddlebags.

She went through the bags very carefully watching her captives and got out supplies for herself, letting Tuff replace the materials she didn't want back into the saddlebags.

Having already taken their guns away, she turned toward Tuff and said, "I will turn the horses loose tomorrow. You may stay here for this or you may leave, on foot with no guns, just your clothes on your back. What's your decision?"

He said, "I deserve a bullet, ma'am."

She said, "No, they do. You have a choice."

He said, "Ma'am, ah'm plumb sorry. I kin promise ya this. Ah'll walk the straight and narrow the rest a mah life."

With that, he turned and walked into the darkness.

Ab yelled after him, "Hey, Tuff, you cain't leave us like this."

Tuff didn't even look back.

She tossed the knife to Ab and said, "Cut his hand off."

He said, "I cain't do thet."

Bond said, "Ef ya do, ah'll kill ya efn' it's the last thing ah ever do."

Ab said, "Shet up. Missy, please now."

Charlotte was holding Tuff's carbine, feeling more confidence with a rifle than a short gun. She pointed the barrel down slightly and fired and Ab grabbed his right thigh muscle, where the bullet burned it. He screamed in pain and hopped up and down holding his leg.

She said, "You aren't hurt that bad, but you will be with the next bullet. Now, you heard me warn him, and you wanted to help. Now, cut off his hand."

Ab grabbed the knife off the ground where he dropped it and walked with a limp to Bond, who screamed and cursed and kicked at him. Ab was convinced, and he just grabbed his partner's arm and quickly sawed away at the left wrist while the other screamed in pain and fury.

Charley said, "Hold it. Use his kerchief and make a tourniquet above it."

Blood was everywhere and Bond passed out cold. Ab quickly finished the job.

She grabbed a canteen and poured water on Bond's head. He came to and looked at his bloody wrist and began sobbing uncontrollably.

Gritting his teeth, he looked at Ab and said, "Ah'm gonna kill you, you sumbitch!"

Charley said, "You two can settle that later."

She walked over to Ab and said, "Turn around."

He whimpered but complied, and she smashed the butt of the rifle into the back of his head. He went down in a heap and Charlotte quickly retrieved another lasso and tied him as tightly as she could, tying off the rope to another tree.

She then busied herself packing her newly

gained supplies and tied the horses' lead lines to the tail of the one ahead and led them off into the darkness, carrying the rifle across the bow of her saddle.

She left Bond back at the trees crying uncontrollably and Ab was in a heap.

As soon as she got out of earshot, Charley started sobbing, too, but she kicked her heels to her horse's side and trotted off to the west, in search of her own destiny.

CHAPTER 2

Land of Enchantment

Taos, New Mexico, lay nestled against piñon and cedar-covered mountains in a very scenic setting. When Charley first laid eyes on the little town, it was from a distance. There was a wagon road that went north from Santa Fe, and it wound along a ridge to the east of, and overlooking, the Rio Grande. Deer grazed along the rushing waters in many places, and the dry summer heat was unforgiving.

Charley watched with awe when the freighter made the last turn around the ridge and she saw the valley sprawled out before her. A couple of years later, her brother would marvel at the very same view.

The mountains were directly to her front, separated from her by a winding flat valley. She could hear the rushing of the whitewater Rio

Grande far below her, but it was out of sight now. Instead, she saw a giant slash in the flat valley floor to her left front. Apparently carved by the Rio Grande, the walls of the gorge went straight down, and she could see the hard rock western walls of the gorge, but the river was too far down in the cut to see. It was an incredible view, running for miles across the valley floor and disappearing into the mountain range to the north that blocked free passage up into Colorado.

"It's beautiful," she marveled.

The white-bearded old man next to her reached into the wooden box of stones at his side and tossed one at the rump of the lead mule and said, "Git up theah, Willy!"

As was his custom, he couldn't quite answer her or respond immediately. He first had to make those with him watch him intently with anticipation until words finally dribbled slowly out of his wind-burned, wrinkled old leather head cover that some folks called a face. He drew some dark brown juice from the big wad of chaw filling his right cheek and spit it at some barrel cactus they passed. Charlotte watched her strange companion intently.

He finally spoke, "Yep, it'll do."

Charlotte laughed again.

She had made her way across Texas and into New Mexico with this old freighter and was still looking for a place to stop and settle down. Texas was a place with bad memories now, and she never wanted to return. She also was concerned that she might at this moment be the victim of a large manhunt trying to track her down for murder. Little did she know how strongly western men, those in and outside the law, felt about molestation of women.

He had picked her up in Abilene, sensing that she was running from something or someone. Two men who owned a saloon were walking beside her as she went down the street trying to pressure her into prostitution. Suddenly, this very large bearded, white-haired teamster, walked up behind them and took her by the arm.

He said, "Awright, gal, we got work ta do."

He pointed toward his large, loaded freight wagon and said, "Go check the diamond hitches on the sideboards and make sure the load's ready ta go."

Shocked but relieved, Charley said, "Yes, sir."

She went straightway to the wagon and pretended like she knew what she was doing.

The old man said to the men, "Now, boys, thet little gal works fer me, and any kinda proposals ya got fer her better come through me. Watcha want?"

One of them said, "Nothing, partner."

The two walked away quickly but turned and watched as the old man walked to the wagon, climbed up on the big bench seat, pulled a stone out of the box, and hit the lead mule on the rump.

"Go on! Giddap!" he growled. "Ya flea-bitten good fer nothin' bunch a bones."

Charlotte said nothing, feeling the stares of the two men on her back. She decided to wait for the old man to speak first. She kept waiting and waiting.

After an hour, the old man spoke, "Gal, Ah'ma headed ta Santa Fe. Yer welcome to ride along and sometimes spell me handlin' the team. Kin ya cook?"

Charlotte said, "Yes."

He said, "Good."

He quit speaking and this surprised her.

They went another hour, and she said, "My name's Charlotte, but my mother called me Charley."

He spat his tobacco juice and said, "Yep."

After five minutes she said, "What's your name?"

He said, "Barnabas Drew, but ya kin call me, Cracker. That's my handle."

Charley said, "How did you get a nickname like that?"

Cracker didn't say a word. He just kept chewing his tobacco and tossing pebbles at the mules.

This was a strange old bird, she thought.

After five minutes, a horsefly landed on the withers of the right rear mule, and the beast's withers twitched spasmodically trying to shoo away the pest.

Cracker's hand suddenly raised up and a long black snake whip uncoiled, and he lashed out with it. There was a loud cracking sound and the horsefly disappeared. The mule was untouched and unstartled. Holding the eight reins in one hand, Cracker expertly coiled up the whip with the other hand and set it down next to him on the big bench.

Charley smiled and looked straight ahead. This man, she concluded, would probably answer most of her questions with action and not words.

She softly said, "Thank you for getting me out of that situation back there."

He nodded and spit out his tobacco.

During the days that followed, Cracker still

hardly spoke and never asked Charley questions about her past. She handled the team more and more frequently as the days wore and made their meals, something he enjoyed quite a bit. He provided her with blankets and a few extra shirts and trousers. Food was plentiful.

Cracker was a very private and withdrawn man, and Charley didn't even know if he liked her or not. She figured he must have or he wouldn't have taken her with him.

He showed her a lot of things and taught her a lot about running a freight wagon.

What really told her a lot about him, though, was when they were crossing western Texas. Some distance north of the famous "Jackass Mail" trail, which ran all the way to San Diego, California, they passed numerous wagons each day. One day, Cracker hailed down one of the other freighters and went off with the man to parley. He apparently knew the man. She saw Cracker hand the man a very beautiful Bowie knife he carried on his waist, which had what looked like ruby and other gems inlaid in the mother of pearl handle. The man admired the knife and nodded and handed Cracker an oil-skin-wrapped parcel.

Later that day, farther down the trail, they

stopped to water and Charley returned from taking care of nature's requirements to find the packet sitting on her side of the bench seat.

Cracker looked straight ahead, clucking to the mules, and explained, "Found that in the back of the wagon. I don't need it. You kin have it."

She unwrapped the oilskin and her eyes opened wide, as Charley looked at a beautiful green dress with white lace trimming all over it. Tears came into her eyes, and she just bent over and started sobbing into her hands. She reached over and hugged him and Cracker was totally taken aback.

He quickly pulled away, clearing his throat and saying, "Here, here. I got to drive the mules, gal. I just give ya that from the wagon. I warn't gonna wear it my own self."

"Right," she replied sarcastically, "anyway, thank you very much, Cracker. You don't know what this means to me."

He said, "Aw, it probably don't even fit."

They rode on for miles without any more words being said.

By the time they reached Santa Fe, Charley had become a pretty good teamster, and she was starting to get pretty knowledgeable about crossing the prairie. She knew how to prepare antelope and bison, what wild plants to look for and how to identify them, and how to make cooking fires by burning dried cattle or bison manure patties.

In Santa Fe, Cracker dropped off the load he carried and picked up a new one to deliver in Taos.

By sunset, the two weary travelers pulled the big freight wagon into the sleepy little town. A small brown dog barked at the two as they climbed down off the wagon. They started toward the little hotel and the dog decided to try "heeling" Cracker, like he had done so many times with the cow creatures. Just as he came up behind the old man to lunge at his Achilles tendon, the teamster wheeled around and spit a big stream of tobacco juice, which hit the startled cur right in the left eye. The mutt gave out with a yelp and ran whining down the street.

Charley chuckled and shook her head at the actions of her mentor.

He calmly said, "Ef yer gonna sneak up and bite sumthin' make sure ya know what yer bitin'."

They walked inside and rented two rooms. Cracker told her to get freshened up and meet him downstairs in half an hour. The first thing Charlotte did, though, was to flop down on the featherbed. She uttered a loud sigh and smiled up at the ceiling. Charlotte removed all of her clothes and poured water in the washbasin. She dipped the washcloth in and started bathing herself all over. It wasn't a bath but anything beat all the days on the dusty and muddy roads and trails. Charley enjoyed Cracker but thought about how nice it would be to live in a town, where she could bathe and change clothes on a regular basis.

She walked down the stairs and met Cracker in the lobby. He whistled as he saw the young lady for the first time in her beautiful dress he had traded for to give to her. She had put her hair up and stuck several daisies in it from the vase in her room.

They walked down the street to a little place called the Bon Ton Cafe, a name that seemed to be used all over the West.

Over a dinner of fresh rainbow trout, potatoes, bread, and fresh vegetables, the two talked about the days on the trail. Cracker could tell that it was something that did not make Charley totally happy, although she was loyal and would do whatever was required to make her way in the world. After the second cup of coffee, they decided to retire for the evening.

They were walking down the street and Cracker said, "Reckon this'd be a good place fer ya ta settle down fer a while. The wagon bench is a rough place fer a woman ta work."

Charlotte immediately got defensive, saying, "I can handle the job."

Cracker laughed, saying, "Thet's fer shore. Never said ya couldn't, gal. Ya hold yer end up right fine. I jest said that it was rough. Ya could find ya a job in a place like this and be able ta dress like ya are right now, plumb beautiful."

Charley blushed saying, "Thank you, Cracker, but I enjoy helping you."

This made Cracker sad, as he knew what he had to do. With that in mind, nothing would deter him from his duty. He reached down in his war bag and pulled out a little sack. Opening it, he pulled out a handful of coins, then handed them to Charley. She was shocked.

"What is this?" she asked shocked.

Cracker said, "A bunch of double eagles."

She said, "But this is a lot of money. What are you doing?"

Cracker grinned, "Wal, I told ya, ya was a good worker. Thet's yer wages. I figgered ya might want ta do some shoppin' tomorrow. We'll be here a few days. Stay in bed in the morning and catch up on your sleep. Then you git you a nice bath, mebbe another dress, and have some fun. We'll get on the trail the next day, or mebbe the next. I', old. I need the rest, too."

Charlotte said, "Thank you, but I didn't ask for wages or money."

Cracker said, "I know, but ya earned it, every penny. It's honest wages. Spend 'em or save 'em. Makes me no nevermind, but it's yer money."

They went into the building and he led the way up the creaking stairway. At their doors he turned and gave her a wink and a big smile.

She said, "Good night."

Cracker half turned his head and gave her a half salute saying, "S'long," and entered his door.

She didn't see the tears. He hid them until he was in his room.

Charley counted her money and smiled as she shook the coins back and forth in her hands and listened to them jingle. She got undressed and looked out the window at the many stars in the clear sky. Taking a deep breath of fresh air, she walked to the bed and fell asleep as soon as her head hit the pillow.

The sun streaked through the window, and the bright light penetrated through Charlotte's eyelids. Her sleep had seemed dreamless, it was so needed and long in coming. She squinted her eyes and stretched out, yawning. Cracker was right; the first thing she was going to do was to head to the tonsorial parlor, or elsewhere, and find a bath. She would take a long leisurely one and even pour some fragrances in the bathwater.

For the first time in months, Charlotte hadn't awakened to a bad dream. She slept the sleep of the dead, her dreams so deep into her subconscious, she was not aware of even dreaming.

Now it was almost midmorning, and she got out of bed feeling refreshed and rested, almost renewed. She wondered if Cracker was still sleeping. He always worked so hard and never seemed tired, hungry, sick, or hurt, but she knew there had been many times on the trail when he was each of those.

She ate a hearty breakfast downstairs in the small cafe, even indulging herself in a large bowl of apple cobbler with fresh cream poured on it. After a second pot of tea, she paid her bill and left to look for a bath.

The bathhouse was just two buildings down the street and Charley enjoyed herself thoroughly. She soaked for an hour and shampooed her hair twice, brushing it out until she thought she would wear the bristles off the brush. Returning to her room, she changed into her dress, and set off looking for Cracker.

The first place she checked was the livery stable, and was taken aback when she didn't see the team in the stalls where he had checked them in. Nobody was around, but she did hear someone whistling in the corral. Charley started to panic a little bit and rushed around the livery checking all the stalls. She was almost afraid to go out to the corral and speak with the whistler, but she finally did so.

The man in the corral was shoveling manure out of a wooden wheelbarrow with steel wheels. He would take small scoops and toss them onto a large pile of manure in the edge of the corral. His hair was very sparse and very short, and he had a long handlebar mustache with drooping ends and lots of gray in it.

Charlotte said, "Sir, there was a freighter who brought his team and rig in here yesterday."

The man interrupted, "Yah, and right you are, missy. That would be Cracker. He left out of here early this morning before daybreak. He told me you'd be coming by."

The man had a thick Scandinavian accent, but she didn't notice, she was so upset. Tears flooded her eyes.

Charley inquired, "What did he tell you?"

The man said, "By yiminy, he said you'd be crying, too. He said to tell you that all birds must fly. He said, you'd understand."

Charlotte put her arms over the corral rail and buried her face in them, sobbing.

She said, "I never even got to say good-bye, or thank you."

The livery man said, "Cracker isn't the kind of man who vould let you say good-bye, or thanks, if he cared a lot about you, missy."

Charlotte said, "How far would he have gotten?"

The livery man said, "Not too far. He vas driving a vagon, you know."

Charlotte said, "I want to rent a horse, sir."

The man smiled and said, "Can't do that, missy."

Charley said, "Why not?"

The man replied, "By yiminy, old Cracker thought of that too, he did. He bought my last horse and gave it to the first cowboy that valked by the livery. I asked him vhy he did that, and he said, you'd try to rent it from me. He din't want you ta follow, missy."

Charley softly said, "Thank you," turned and walked away, still crying.

The man ran after her, saying, "Missy, missy."

Charley turned, wiping away the tears. She gave him a questioning look.

He smiled and said, "Cracker said to tell you that all birds think they cannot fly vhen they leave the nest, but they yust have to spread dere wings and yust flap them."

Charlotte understood his reasoning and smiled at the comment, but she still felt empty inside. She went back to her hotel room and had a good cry, lying across the featherbed. She then realized that Cracker was one chapter in her life that was now past, and it was time to move on to new places and new things.

She went downstairs and ordered dinner, enjoying frijoles, refried beans, and rice, along with a pot of coffee. She then walked down the street, looking for "help wanted" signs. There was a small newspaper, and she bought a copy, taking it back to the restaurant. She ordered some more coffee and a large slice of pie, while she read through the paper.

The only advertisement she found was from

another town, Cimarron. She knew nothing about the town or where it was located, but the ad was for a hotel clerk at the St. James Hotel. At the time, Charley did not know that the St. James had provided housing for a number of famous travelers. Wyatt and Morgan Earp stayed there, as well as Wyatt's friends Doc Holliday and Bat Masterson. Also staying there was Governor Lew Wallace, who pardoned Billy the Kid, and Sheriff Pat Garrett, who shot Billy the Kid. There were many other famous and colorful characters who stayed in the hotel, but the reason they did was, because it was a very wild and colorful place. There were numerous gunfights and killings that had gone on there and the notorious St. James was the hub of activity in the raucous town of Cimarron.

The bartender was cleaning glasses at the mahogany-top bar when Charlotte walked up to him and said, "Sir, can you tell me how far it is to Cimarron?"

"Yep," he said, as he breathed fog on glass and gave it an extra shine.

After a pregnant pause, he went on, "Two days' ride, But, efn' yer hard-pressed it's jest a one-day hard ride northeast ef'n yer on a horse with some bottom to it. Ya jest taken the road ta Raton, an ye'll git there."

Thanking him, Charlotte went out the door and headed down the street to the stage office. She booked passage on the one leaving the next morning.

Following this, she decided to walk to the small cafe down the street and have a cup of tea. She noticed a man and woman who looked like they were hardworking ranchers. There was something different about the woman, though, and then Charley noticed it. She was quite pregnant and seemed to be having a rough time moving items around in the buckboard. A small cur barked at the man while he loaded supplies onto the back of the wagon.

It looked to Charlotte as if the two had every item they owned packed in the wagon, and she was about to find out it was an accurate estimate. She stopped and crawled up onto the bench seat and helped the woman move a bag of flour behind the bench. The woman smiled softly and a little tear formed in the far corner of her left eye. Charlotte smiled to herself as she recalled how sensitive some women would become when they were carrying a child.

Charlotte placed the bag in the proper spot

and started to climb down off the wagon seat, but the woman gently laid a hand on her forearm.

With a trace of a Georgia accent, the woman said, "That was so kind of you. Thank you ever so much."

Charlotte smiled, "My pleasure. How soon is the baby due?"

The woman said, "One or two more months, but it feels like it could be tomorrow. My husband just inherited a small ranch outside Cimarron and we are on our way there now."

"Cimarron," Charlotte said, excited. "You know I am booked on tomorrow's stage to Cimarron, but I would be happy to cash in my ticket if you would like my help on the way."

The woman said, "I would love your help, Miss, but even if the stage doesn't leave until tomorrow, you would still get to Cimarron much quicker than us."

Charley said, "I know, but you need help, and I would love to save every penny I can."

The woman looked at her husband, and he smiled and nodded.

She smiled and said, "Well, welcome, Miss, and thank you for your consideration."

Charley said, "Thank you for taking me. I was

not looking forward to the trip on the stage anyway. Too confining. I have been working on a freight wagon for some time now, and I can easily help handle your team, too."

The man said, "That's music to my ears, Miss. There's so much to do on the trail, and I can sure use the extra hands so the missus can relax and take care. Name's Jedediah Adamson. My wife here is Mary Katherine."

Charley nodded at the man and shook hands with the wife, saying, "My name is Charlotte Colt, but my mother always called me Charley. Please do?"

The man said, "You can call me Jed, but Mary Katherine prefers the whole name proper. She's from Atlanta."

Mary Katherine blushed and said, "It will be so nice to have another woman to talk to, so I don't have to listen to such dribble."

The man grinned and checked the large water barrel on the side of the wagon. Charley smiled as she climbed down from the bench.

She said, "I'll be right back. I'm going to ask for a refund on my stagecoach ticket."

On the way back, Charlotte stopped at the mercantile, and using a good bite out of the funds left her by Cracker, she bought a Smith

and Wesson Pocket .32-caliber single-action revolver. It was used but had been well taken care
of, but the shoulder holster with it had a torn
shoulder strap. She also bought two pouches of
bullets for it without knowing how many were
in each pouch. She just asked the merchant to
throw it in, and batted her eyes, and they were
hers. Charley selected the gun because the
smaller caliber would not kick as much, but she
did not know that this particular gun was a favorite backup gun of many shootists.

Charlotte knew how to shoot because of her
experiences hunting and practicing in case she
would ever have had to shoot her stepfather. She
hoped she would not need it, but had the feeling
that the time had come in her life, where she
should have a gun with her for protection.

The three spent the night a good distance outside of Taos. They staked a tarp out from the side
of the buckboard and slept in bedrolls on the
long mountain grasses.

In the morning, Charley wouldn't let Mary
Katherine get out of her bedroll. She insisted she
stay there and relax, while Charley built the
cooking fire and made coffee, sausage, and corn
fritters with molasses. Jed ate three helpings and
patted his stomach with great satisfaction. Mary

Katherine ate for two, as usual. She and Jed were both very impressed with Charlotte, watching her work around their little makeshift camp, cleaning the dishes, ensuring the fire was totally extinguished, then burying the ashes under dirt, explaining that you can never be too careful with a cooking fire, especially with trees around.

They were on the road again shortly after daybreak and had not gone more than a quarter of a mile when they heard the pounding of hoofbeats coming down off the ridge to their immediate south. Charley was shocked and frightened when she saw eight Indian warriors riding toward them at a fast trot. All were armed and they did not look very friendly.

Suddenly, Mary Katherine grabbed her abdomen and moaned in pain. Her mouth twisted with the pain and panic, as well. Jed, looking at the approaching warriors, grabbed his Henry and stopped the team. Charley reached over, grabbed the rifle and his pouch of bullets, and jumped down on the ground.

"Your wife is having your child," Charley commanded. "Get out of here while I stall them."

He looked at his wife, then Charlotte, and started to argue, but Charley slapped the rear steed on the rump, with a curse, and the team took off at a gallop.

Charley turned to face the Apaches, her newly acquired rifle held across her body, finger on the trigger. She could hear the wagon tearing away around the bend and the group of warriors split apart to pursue. Charlotte immediately pulled the rifle up to her shoulder and fired two quick shots in front of the lead ponies in both groups. The group on the left slid to a stop, but the one on the right kept on.

She shouldered the rifle and took careful aim and put a bullet right through the shoulder of the lead Apache, knocking him off the mount's back. He hit the ground in a heap and came up immediately holding the bloody shoulder and wincing in pain. The other warriors halted, though. Charley jacked another round in the chamber and aimed it at the center of the chest of the leader. That's what she had attempted when she shot the one in the shoulder, but the horse was moving fast.

The leader was tall and wiry with a very muscular body. Most of the warriors were shorter and stocky, but this one was over six feet and looked whipcord tough. He wore leather moccasins that folded like an accordion down around his ankles. When moving through bad cactus and thorn country he would simply pull the upper part up over the calves and be protected from the rough plants in the arid unforgiving mountain and desert country. He also wore a brown breechcloth made of homespun material, and a wide faded red scarf around his forehead for a headband. While the other warriors sat their ponies, he swung his leg over the mane of his dirty little Palomino and slid down. The leader walked toward the beautiful young woman, with a menacing look on his square-jawed face.

"I *will* put a bullet through your chest big enough to bake a loaf of bread in," she spoke.

The Apache understood English, but more importantly, he understood the look in her eyes. He stopped about eight feet in front of her. The one who had been shot in the shoulder moaned. The leader gave him a nasty look and said some words in Apache that Charlotte couldn't make out. She figured, though, that he must have scolded the man, because the wounded brave let go of his shoulder and arched his back, sticking his chin out proudly. Stoic in his demeanor, he stood perfectly erect and another whimper did not escape from his lips.

Charley was frightened, probably more so than ever in her life, but Cracker had told her all about Indians, and especially the Apache. She knew these were Apache by their dress and the area they were in. She figured that they must be from the Jicarilla tribe. She also knew that Apaches especially very much respected courage. It was said that a white man Tom Jeffords had ridden to the rancheria of the mighty Cochise, who had killed numerous white men and was able to start a friendship that ended up with a truce between the white man and many of the Apaches.

She spoke, "I thought the Apache were warriors. I did not know that they had nothing between their legs and made war against women."

She saw the leader's lips tighten up with anger.

He said, "We do not make war against women. Who are you to speak of these things to the Jicarilla?"

She didn't answer, but instead said, "Who are you, brave fighter of women?"

He said, "I am Gahe of the Jicarilla. What are you called, woman of the sharp tongue?"

She said, "My name is Charley."

He said, "That is a white man's name. Not a woman's name."

She said, "If all of you men fight against one woman alone, maybe Gahe is a woman's name."

His temper started to flare up again, but he caught himself and smiled. He was very impressed with this fiery beautiful white woman. Nevertheless, he and his men had an important mission to accomplish.

Gahe said, "A white-eyes took the wife of my brother and made her lay with him. He cut her breasts and cut her face."

He made cutting gestures with his finger indicating how she had been cut.

Gahe said, "Maybe we will make you lay with us, white woman with a man's name."

Charley heard that her brother had an outstanding reputation among whites and Indians alike, so she thought she'd try the name and see what effect it would have.

She said, "My name is Charlotte, which is a woman's name. My last name is Colt."

It definitely had the desired effect. She saw it in his face.

She continued, "And you may have a hard time getting me to lay with you, since you'll all be dead."

Gahe said, "You talk big, but you cannot kill all of us, even if you are the wife of Colt."

She said, "I am his sister, not his wife. And I probably cannot kill you all, but I will kill you first, and a few of your friends."

She was exhilarated. She could not believe she was acting so bravely in the face of such danger, but she was angry at their intrusion and she had no other choice anyway.

Gahe spoke with the others, and she heard the name Colt mentioned several times. One man came forward, with a very cocky sneer on his chiseled brown face. He held an old Starr Double-Action Army .44 revolver and seemed ready to use it.

Gahe explained, "He says no woman will speak to him the way you spoke. He tells you to take off your dress for him."

She hesitated and the brave quickly aimed and fired, and she grabbed her left arm. A bloody crease appeared across her forearm. Charley's eyes welled up with tears, and she sobbed.

Gahe seemed to give the brave an angry look, but he ordered, "He speak, lay down rifle."

She resignedly dropped her rifle to the ground and slowly reached down and grabbed the bottom of her dress. She started to raise it up, exposing her very muscular and shapely legs. Above her knees, she reached up under the dress as the braves watched, several literally licking their lips.

Suddenly, her hand came out from under the dress and in it was her .32 she had bought. She cocked the gun while pulling it from the garter and fired it into the chest of the startled brave with the .44. He looked down at the large red spot on his chest, and he looked at the big stream of blood spurting out three feet in front of him from the hole. His eyes crossed and his legs suddenly went limp.

The brave fell on the ground, and he looked at the pool of blood soaking into the ground in front of his eyes. He tried to understand why he was becoming so sleepy. Then a chill ran up and down his spine. He realized he had been shot and was dying. He tried to sing his death song, but he couldn't make his mouth work and his chest felt like a horse was standing on it. He tried to ask Gahe for help, but he couldn't make words come out. He couldn't move his eyes anymore, and he suddenly, vividly, remembered the first rabbit he killed as a boy. He had thrown a lance and really accidentally pierced the animal's lungs. He remembered now the look in the rabbit's eyes as the life drained out of it. He remembered how the eyes quit moving around, and he just stared at them. Then the breathing stopped, and the eyes started glazing over on the little hare. That image was with him, and he suddenly couldn't breathe anymore. He panicked and felt abject terror. Everything got dark, and the brave wanted to scream, but then everything faded out.

Charley felt a wave of sadness as she saw the warrior's chest fail to rise for the last time. She knew that she had to take a hard stand, though, or she would be violated first, then dead. She bent over and picked up the rifle, replacing the gun under her dress with her left hand. She then walked over to the brave and yanked out his knife, cutting a strip of white material from her petticoat. Using her teeth and right hand, she bound her flesh wound and tied it off. The bleeding was minimal but it really hurt. She blocked the pain from her mind.

Gahe said, "You have shot two of my men. That one is dead. How many will I let you shoot, before you die?"

She said, "That depends on how many try to shoot me first."

Gahe said, "We will not kill you, unless you shoot again."

Charley said, "What do you want?"

Gahe said, "I spoke of this."

Charlotte said, "The people I was with, the man, he is not the man you look for. Why don't you tell the cavalry about this man?"

Gahe laughed. "Why do I not shoot an arrow at that mountain yonder and make a deer roll down and lay at my feet?"

He went on, "If some man lay with you and cut you like this, would your man not kill him? Would his brother and cousin not kill him also? Your brother would do such a thing, I know."

"Maybe my brother would," she replied, "but there has been a lot of trouble between the whites and Apaches. This could cause more. I have no man, and my brother is far away."

Gahe replied, "He lives in the valley of the mountains of rain. Your brother is a great warrior and is respected by Cochise, Geronimo, and many of our peoples. The white-eyes should have thought of the troubles between our people when they violated the wife of my brother. We are not children to be scolded and punished by the white fathers. We are Apache."

Charlotte said, "You make a good point."

Charley just wanted to keep talking and stall for time to let the expectant couple get as far away as possible. Her arm burned like the dickens.

Gahe said, "Why do you not have a man? Was he killed in battle?"

Charley blushed and said, "I am not ready for a man yet. I am still young."

There were plenty of young ladies who had married a lot earlier than Charley, but she meant it. She wasn't ready to even consider marriage, yet. She did notice how men looked at her whenever she walked by. She knew, at home, there were probably several young men who would love to marry her if she would have just given them a sign. Charlotte was in no hurry, though, and would wait until the right man came along, and she was not about to rush it. The way Gahe now looked at her, she figured he was thinking he was the right man.

He said, "You need a good man. You will come and live in the wickiup of Gahe."

She said, "No, I will not."

He said, "Where will you go now? You have no pony?"

She said, "Yes, I do."

She looked down at the Apache she killed and said, "Where is his pony? It is now mine."

Gahe smiled and said something over his shoulder. Another brave brought a pony forward, handing the braided leather war bridle to Charley.

She had heard somewhere, probably Cracker, she figured, that Indians did not say "thank you," so she just nodded and half smiled.

Gahe said, "We eat now. You will come to our rancheria and eat and sleep. The mother of Gahe will treat your wound. You will be safe. Then you can go on after your friends. You are truly the sister of the mighty Colt."

Just hearing that excited her. She had heard more and more stories about her half-brother Chris Colt, who she still had not met. He was becoming legendary. She could not wait to someday meet him.

This was a time when most people never traveled more than twenty-five miles from the place where they were born. Most people never heard an orchestra in their entire lives, and most people only read four books over the course of their existence. One out of every four family members died from smallpox, cholera, or some other epidemic. So, Charlotte probably would not have visited Chris anytime soon, even though he lived less than 175 miles north of her in Colorado.

Charlotte suddenly felt light-headed, and she quickly steeled herself. She reasoned that she was just frightened or shocked because of the wound and tried to rationalize her safety. She did start becoming more clear-headed, when she thought it through and knew she hadn't lost more than a few drops of blood and her wound was not life-threatening. It was a shock to the system, though, just being shot. It also was now hurting a lot more, but again she tried to block the pain out of her mind as much as possible.

Charlotte decided to accompany the band of Apaches to their rancheria and get treated. Cracker had told her about the honesty of most warriors, although there were bad apples in every society. He had also told her about healing from near-death because of a band of Kwahhaddy Comanches taking him in on the Staked Plain one time and treating his wounds with herbs and poultices that seemed to be miraculous in their curative powers.

She rode third in line behind Gahe, while a small-point element of just one brave rode ahead of the rest to watch for and warn of dangers on the trail. Nobody spoke on the journey, so Charlotte simply rode. She saw earlier that the Apaches nodded in approval when she grabbed a handful of mane and swung up onto the pony's back, then immediately rode him, easily controlling him while holding the single rein from the war bridle and primarily using knee and calf pressure to control the lithe little gelding.

Gahe admired her and looked at the expedient bandage wrapped around her forearm. He thought to himself that she was indeed a warrior woman. He thought she probably could gather more firewood more quickly than others, cook better, and would keep a cleaner wickiup. On top of all that, he concluded, looking at her beauty, she would be wonderful to lie beside at night. He figured that the brave who had her in his bed would not sleep much each night but would always be smiling.

Charley glanced at Gahe and noticed again how the warrior had been looking at her. She was uncomfortable and couldn't wait to get away from these people. She had heard how much honor there was among the Indians of all tribes and how rare lying was, and he had given his word that she was safe among his people. She believed that, but on the other hand, she knew how men could be when they looked at her like that. Her stepfather had taught her that lesson early and made her grow up a little too quickly.

Their rancheria was not the same as what she had pictured. There were little lodges, called wickiups, made of branches woven together in an igloo shape and brush interwoven through the framework. What did look different to her, was that the rancheria did not seem like a civilization center but more like an outlaw hideout. That was, in fact, almost what it was. Gahe saw her looking at the sentries coming down off the rocks and the narrow, high mountain gulch the rancheria was hidden in.

He explained, "We must hide here. Our home is at Bosque Redondo, but we leave. Find man who did bad thing to sister woman. The white-eyes not ask us go, find, and kill men."

"Where do you get water from?" she asked.

"There is a tank. There," he said, "between those trees."

He pointed, indicating twin cottonwood trees.

A number of women and children emerged from the wickiups and came forward, looking curiously at Charlotte. The band split apart, and she followed Gahe to a wickiup in the center of the group. A stocky gray-haired woman came forward flashing a smile up at Gahe. He dismounted and accepted a gourd of water from her. He spoke a few words in Apache, and she walked over to the spring and filled the gourd with more water and handed it to Charley. The young woman smiled and drank the water, walked over to the tank, and refilled it twice more.

It was an hour before Gahe sat down and spoke with his mother, and she kept looking across the wickiup at the white woman. She then left the wickiup, and Gahe spent most of the time eating and resting, with a lot of stares at Charlotte. She dozed off and came awake with a start. Charley sat up and saw the brave fast asleep across the lodge from her.

Finally, the old woman came in the door carrying several plants and what looked like some tree sap. Charlotte watched with interest as the woman hummed a song, and using a stone mortar and pestle, ground several of the plants into powder, which was mixed with the sap and heated. When the poultice was ready, she applied it to the wound on Charley's arm and there was instant relief. She smiled at the old woman, who grinned back at her.

Charlotte lay back, and the next thing she knew, her eyes opened up, and it was morning. Nobody else was in the wickiup. There was a fire going and the wickiup was warm and cozy. Charlotte got up and stretched pleased with the mobility and relative lack of pain in her wounded arm.

She walked outside into the morning sunlight and was totally shocked. She looked all around in every direction and saw a giant white blanket of snow almost a foot deep, with more snowflakes swirling down. Apache women appeared walking from the trees with large armfuls of firewood and carried them to different wickiups. It was late summer, and Charlotte could not believe what had happened. She didn't understand all the snow, but she did understand shared responsibility and survival. Shivering from the cold, she half walked and half trotted toward the distant trees and started breaking off dry branches from the trees. She soon had a large-size pile of wood and carried the bundle back to the wickiup. As she started to leave the lodge, she ran into the old woman who was carrying an even larger armful of wood herself.

Her arm did not bother her very much at all, and she ended up carrying five more loads of wood to the wickiup. It was obvious to her that the old woman appreciated the extra help.

Gahe showed up just after dark carrying a small doe over his shoulder. The old woman immediately took over the task of skinning and gutting it. He sat down and ate a bowl of stew that was waiting for him. Charlotte also ate a gourdful of the foul-smelling concoction.

After eating, as was Apache custom, Gahe wiped his hands on his arms and lit a pipe, not a peace pipe, but a white man's corncob pipe. He blew the smoke toward the smoke hole at the top of the wickiup.

Charlotte waited for him to speak first.

She didn't have to wait long, as Gahe said, "Snow comes early. Tomorrow, much more."

Charley said, "More? But I have to leave. I have to go to Cimarron!"

Gahe said, "You will stay here, until the snow goes away and fills the bellies of all the rivers and streams."

She was angry now and said, "I can't wait that long! I have to go."

Gahe said quietly, "I do not want to stay here, but Mother Earth speaks to us with cold words. We listen to Mother Earth, or we die. The snow came early. We are high in the mountains and cannot escape. We will stay. If you want to die, leave and die."

Charlotte had learned one thing a long time ago and it had proven her well so far. And that was to be a survivor.

Something her mother said to her one time had stuck with her all her life. Charlotte had fallen from her horse while practicing an equestrian event and had broken her leg. She was supposed to compete the next month and her mother came into her room and found the young girl crying. When she asked what was wrong, Charlotte explained that her chances were ruined for winning any event, and she was really upset.

Her mother held her in her soft hands and looked into her daughter's beautiful eyes, saying, "Charley, I want you to remember something, for the rest of your life. What happens to us is totally inconsequential. Sometimes it's inconvenient, or even horrible, but it's inconsequential. What is really important, Charley, my dear, is how we react to what happens to us."

Those words had stuck with Charlotte probably more than anything her mother had ever told her. She didn't even understand the word inconsequential at the time, but she looked it up in the dictionary so she would. From that first conversation, she had an attitude to come out on top, no matter what. She was indeed a survivor and a winner. This was proven when she rode in the equestrian event with a broken leg and took second place to the applause of all the spectators.

Charley looked across the lodge at Gahe and said, "I will find a lodge to sleep in where there's an unmarried woman."

Gahe said, "We call home wickiup. You stay here with mother of Gahe. Her name is Nalin. Gahe stays in wickiup of brother of Gahe."

Charley said, "That is not right. This is your home."

Gahe smiled. "Gahe does not say, Fox, get young chicken and tell it to sleep in your den, but don't eat chicken."

Charlotte got the message and was very relieved that he had taken such an attitude. She had learned several valuable lessons, and one important one was that the mountains were beautiful and majestic but could kill you if you didn't respect them. In the few days that followed, she saw clearly what Gahe meant when he told her essentially that they were stuck up in the mountains. She would survive and do her part around the rancheria, but she would maintain her dignity.

*   *   *

It was late spring and the snow was melting up in the distant mountains. The streams and rivers were running full to the tops of their banks, and one of the neighbor's horses had drowned trying to cross a white-water stream.

Mary Katherine Adamson looked out the window, past the well and the big old wooden bucket and dipper. Jed had been in the field checking the feed corn, but was not heading quickly toward the house. She got concerned and automatically ran to the crib and looked down at her baby daughter. The little tyke was sleeping soundly. Mary Katherine immediately ran to the mantel and grabbed the Spencer rifle and met him at the door.

He ran in and took the rifle from her hands, saying simply, "Apache."

Mary Katherine looked out the door and saw a lone Apache rider coming toward their cabin. The rider carried a carbine and was mounted on a small buckskin pony with a leather bridle and simple blanket on it. The Apache wore the traditional over-the-calf moccasins, breechcloth, and a sunfaded blue shirt with a necklace over that. The Apache also wore a six-shooter tucked into the waistband.

Mary Katherine's heart started pounding, but she felt secure with Jedediah around, although he hadn't seemed quite the same ever since they were forced to leave the lovely Charlotte Colt to the mercy of the Indians. After Mary Katherine was safely away and the baby delivered at the side of a mountain stream, he had broken down and cried right in front of her. After his father died of the pox, he had broken down once in their barn and she walked in on him, but that was the only time she had ever seen Jedediah crying. He had tried bravely to hold it back, after they left Charley, but he just could not do it. When he broke down, it was as if the dam burst. It made Mary Katherine cry even harder, because she knew her proud husband had felt he had deserted a woman and left her to torture and slow death. Mary Katherine, on the other hand, felt bad about Charley's death, but she didn't blame her husband at all. Instead, she focused on the gratitude she felt toward the memory of Charlotte Colt.

Jedediah's finger tightened slightly on the trigger as he aimed at the approaching Apache. Inside, he wanted to make up for what had happened to the brave young woman who had risked her life to save theirs and their baby. The brave kept riding nonchalantly forward and Jed, still a moral man who could not just fire from ambush, did not pull the trigger. The Apache pulled up to the hitching rack in front of the bar and dismounted, but led the pony to the corral, removed the war bridle and blanket and draped them over the corral bars. The brave then turned toward the house, carrying the carbine loosely by the stock.

Jed said over his shoulder, "Brazen son of a buck."

Mary Katherine stayed back, her eyes searching the room for another weapon. They fell on a fireplace poker, and she grabbed it in her hand, clutching it tightly.

There was a knock on the door and the couple looked at each other.

Jed said, "Unfriendly injuns don't knock on doors. Stay behind the door and open it slowly."

He moved back to the other side of the room and raised his rifle, cocking it, and he aimed at the center of the door. The ten feet Mary Katherine walked to the door was the longest distance in her life. She stood behind the door as Jedediah had said and carefully, slowly lifted the latch. She opened the door and wished she could see through it. Instead, she watched Jed's face. That shocked her even more as his eyes filled with tears, and his mouth dropped open. The rifle lowered slowly, almost automatically, and he subconsciously uncocked it, before dropping it at his feet.

Mary Katherine couldn't believe this reaction and she peered around the door and right into the teary eyes of Charlotte Colt.

Mary Katherine screamed, "Praise the Lord!"

She threw herself into Charley's arms and the two women hugged, laughed, and cried for several full minutes. Jedediah's legs gave out on him, and he almost fell back into a rocking chair and lowered his face into his hands, sobbing quietly.

When he stood, a smiling Charlotte walked up to him and paused, then she stepped forward and wrapped him in a powerful hug.

He said, "Charlotte, I, I . . ."

Charley laughed, saying, "You have nothing to explain, if that is what you're attempting. You had no choice back then. You had a wife and baby to protect. The stage driver who gave me directions told me you have a daughter, so where is she?"

Mary Katherine cried again and ran into the

little side room and emerged carrying the infant in her arms and walked over to Charley.

Mary Katherine said proudly, "We named her Charlotte, but we call her Charley."

Charlotte again welled up with tears and kissed the baby on the forehead.

"She's beautiful," Charley whispered with a husky voice.

She stayed with them for two weeks before heading into Cimarron to find work. Mary Katherine generously altered three of her own dresses and gave them to Charley, as well as the young lady's war bag, which had been left with the fleeing wagon.

The St. James Hotel was large and was still under construction. The lights from the hotel were bright and the tinpanny music and raucous noise permeated the streets of Cimarron, even being heard from blocks away. It was very obviously the center of activity in Cimarron, at least after dark. Charley was a little shocked at the St. James, but registered for a room without incident and retired for the evening. She had come into town twice before with the couple but had not really entered the hotel, nor had she seen it after dark. It was wild in the hotel saloon.

The next morning, Charlotte traveled the main street of the rough town and found a small cafe that was crowded. That could only mean good food, so she entered and ate a hearty breakfast.

The food was good and the price reasonable. The young woman knew she would be eating a lot of meals there. She left and walked leisurely back to the hotel, getting lots of stares from men on the way. Charley had gotten lots of sunshine during her stay with the Apaches, and her lovely skin had a golden glow to it now, which just emphasized her already-beautiful features.

When she returned to the hotel, she went straightaway to her room, noticing that the desk clerk was dozing behind the register desk.

Going down the hallway, she couldn't help but notice the layer of dust on the flowered wallpaper, nor could she miss hearing the sounds of a commotion from the direction of her room. Charley, not one to hesitate now when there was trouble brewing, picked up the pace and headed to her room. As she stormed down the hallway, she noticed that her room door was open and she could hear the sounds of at least two drunken men in the room, laughing and breaking things.

She turned quickly and headed downstairs. No one was in sight, so she headed into the bar and the ten patrons, piano player, and bartender all stopped and stared at her as she entered the forbidden area. The hotel manager leaned against the bar where he had been engaging in some gossip with the barkeep in the dirty, white ruffled shirt. Charley walked up to him, an angry look on her face.

She said, "Sir, am I to assume you are the manager of this establishment?"

He cleared his throat, straightened his shoulders, and replied, "Yes, ma'am."

Jaws clenched tightly, she said, "Then, sir, can you tell me why there are drunken hooligans in my room right now?"

He shuffled his feet and looked nervously at the bartender, saying finally, "Ah, I don't rightly know, ma'am, but Ah'm shore they're just some cowboys blowing off steam. Why don't we jest let 'em cool down a mite?"

Furious, Charlotte turned on her heel and stormed out of the saloon. Not stopping, she went through the lobby and up the dirty stairwell. The noises of the drunken cowpunchers still echoed down the hallway, and this set her off even more.

Charley walked into the room to catch one of the two large men with a pair of her daintiest undergarment pulled over his head. She flushed and spotted the other one seated in the corner, a bottle of whiskey in his hand, and laughing uproariously. It took several seconds before they realized she had stepped into the room.

The one with the bottle and the dirty red hair and beard saw her first and stared. The other one noticing this, stopped dancing around with the lace underwear and stared, too. Suddenly, he pointed at her and started laughing again, then his partner joined in. Both men held their sides pointing at her and laughing, but their laughter subsided as she calmly walked over to the nightstand and picked up the water pitcher out of the basin. Neither man could figure out what she was doing as she poured the water from the pitcher into the washbasin.

Then, holding the handle of the pitcher firmly in one hand, she spun around and swung it with a backhand with as much strength as she could muster. The pitcher crashed across the side of the face of the man wearing her panties, and he folded up as if something suddenly made all the bones in his body disappear in an instant.

She faced the other man, and he looked at the man on the floor, clawing for his pistol. She threw the handle of the pitcher at his head, and he ducked while backpedaling, tripping backward over the footstool. While he tried to get back up and grab the gun, she dropped to the floor and pulled the other man's gun from his belt. Using both hands, she cocked it, and the other looked up at the end of the barrel, which right about then looked like the end of a cannon. He only had his own gun halfway out of the holster, but he let go as if he had grabbed a buzz tail with rabies. He raised his hands slowly and stood there, wobbly-legged waiting to find out what his fate would be.

Using the gun, she indicated his friend and said, "Pick him up over your shoulder."

"Yesh, ma'am," he slurred.

He struggled with the limp man and after falling twice, he finally got him across his giant shoulder. He stopped at the doorway, while she still held the gun on him, and he turned.

There was a mean snarl on his ugly face, when he said, "Lady, ya jest made a big mistake. I'll be back, an we'll have us a party. Heah?"

She walked forward, staring into the big man's eyes. Suddenly, he felt a fury welling up inside of him, and he dropped his partner on the floor with a thud.

The behemoth spread his legs and pointed a

pickle-size index finger at her, and started to speak, but she snapped.

Charley dropped the six-shooter on the floor and reached up, grabbing the finger with her right hand and twisted it downward. The man, in pain, spread his fingers apart, and she grabbed his little finger with her other hand. She held onto both fingers and spread them apart, bending his wrist backward and down. She just was angry and grabbed the finger, then the other. She did it because she could tell that it was causing him great pain.

Charlotte didn't stop with that, with the big man dancing on his tiptoes, she held onto her grip and marched him down the hall, the stairway, and across the lobby. Everyone in the saloon was in total shock when she paraded the big man across the smoky room, and they saw the expression of pain on his face. They were all cowboys, ranchers, townspeople, and soldiers in the crowded place. A chuckle broke out as they saw the wincing and inability to speak on his part. She marched him right up to the manager and held him at arm's length.

Charlotte said, "Well, what are you going to do about a big brute who assaults women?"

The laughter stopped abruptly and about a

half-dozen men immediately rose to their feet, with the rest following milliseconds later.

In the frontier West, there were thousands, millions of men and very few women. Women, in the eyes of men, were a rare commodity, like water, but much more important. When pioneers first started traveling west, a code developed and that was to treat women like precious gems. The code remained, even after women started coming to the frontier in droves, as did men. There were cases of outlaws hanging or shooting their own kind for molesting or assaulting a woman.

When Charlotte made her statement, it got the attention of every man in the room.

The silence in the room was finally broken by someone's voice, saying, "Someone get a rope."

The big man's eyes opened as wide as if he just stared into the face of Satan.

Charley said, "He probably deserves it for other things, but I mean he was just drunk and tried to get mean with me. He didn't touch me."

A well-dressed man walked over to her, as half the men sat down and there was the sound of mumbling in the room. He stood by her smiling and just listened.

Charley didn't pay attention to anyone but the hotel manager, saying angrily, "He and his partner destroyed my things and would have destroyed me, no thanks to you. What are you going to do about it?"

The well-dressed man doffed his derby, saying, "Ma'am, what would you do if you were him?"

She looked at the man and said, "The first thing I would do is fire this incompetent, cowardly nincompoop."

The man said, "Well, ma'am, go ahead."

She said, "Pardon me?"

The man pulled out a roll of bills and handed her a wad of them, explaining, "I own this hotel, and you are the new manager if you want the job, with my sincere apologies for your inconvenience and aggravation."

She stared at him for a few seconds, released the big man's fingers as he dashed for the door, and grinned at the old manager.

Charley said, "You're fired. Clear out, now."

The man started to protest, and she pointed at the door.

The big man never made it to the door, as an even bigger man, a cowpuncher, stepped out and hammered him with a thundering right hook to the jaw.

The man hit the floor with a crash on his back,

and the big puncher said to his unconscious frame, "Pardner, ya don't even look at a lady cross-eyed round these parts. If ya do, ye'll have an early demise due to a horrible case of hemp fever."

Two other men walked over to him, tossed a pitcher of beer on his face, and while he sputtered and choked, tossed him unceremoniously through the front window. One of them walked over to the neatly dressed hotel owner and handed him several coins. The cowboy then tipped his hat at Charley and returned to his table.

In the meantime, the fired manager meekly walked through the door into the lobby.

Two days later, the hotel looked like a new place. Every room had been rewallpapered, almost. The hallway walls and ceiling had been scrubbed thoroughly with soap and water and plans were underway to repaper those walls, too. Charlotte found that if she smiled just right and asked the right way, there were plenty of out-of-work cowboys who were more than happy to do work for her for the delicious home-cooked meals she started serving up in the hotel kitchen.

After six months, the hotel had become a very popular place. People would come up from Taos, over from Raton, and even down from Trinidad to spend a day or two at the St. James in Cimarron. Charlotte was excellent at managing it and was great at motivating people to do what she needed. She accepted the fact that it was a wild place with a wild reputation, so she built on that but still tried to maintain reasonable controls.

It was also after six months that the big man she threw out of her room and his partner decided enough time had passed for them to exact revenge against her.

The big man was named Dub Rupert, and his smaller, but still sizable saddle partner, was named Renny Gilchrist. He was not all there, sense-wise.

Dub was just plain, blinded-rattlesnake mean. He had been raised by an abusive uncle after both parents disappeared in a late-spring blizzard on the plains of North Dakota Territory. The uncle wanted Dub for one reason only and that was free labor. A big man, the uncle would stand for no guff by anybody, especially a "snot-nosed kid." The abuse continued until Dub was twelve years old, and the lad decided one day to take the thick end of a hard ash ax handle to his napping uncle. With his pent-up fury finally coming out, the boy made more permanent sleeping arrangements for the mean old man. After that, he spent some hard years raising himself, and as would be expected, he made quite a few bad decisions, and ended up on the owl-hoot trail by the age of fifteen. By that time, he was starting to make hard cash, either backshooting people for a price or beating them with clubs, along with his sizable fists and feet. He could have, in fact, accumulated a nice nest egg, but he enjoyed hurting people too much.

His saddle partner wasn't quite as bad, but he was bad enough.

Charlotte had convinced old William Burwall to build her a small barn and attached chicken coop out behind the hotel, and she kept a couple dairy cows and a bunch of laying hens. The milk and eggs were always fresh for the hotel meals, and the folks around appreciated it. It was early morning, on a sunny Tuesday, when she finished her indoor chores, then went out to the barn for the milking and to the coop for the eggs.

Walking out of the little two-stall barn and around the corner to the fence gate of the chicken coop, Charley stopped short as she came face to face with Dub and Renny. The look on their faces, especially the evil grins, took the breath from her, and the blood literally drained from

her face. She looked into the business end of a
Colt Russian .44 and heard the loud click of it
cocking, as Dub put his finger to his lips and
made a shushing sound.

Her mind started thinking of ways to escape,
but she knew that her chances were slim to none.
If worse came to worse, she would scream, but
she was equally certain that would bring a quick
death by way of bullets. Charlotte thought about
it and figured that might be better than what
these two had planned. She knew that, at the end
of it, there would be slow, painful death. She had
them thrown out of town, almost lynched, and
humiliated in front of a bunch of other men. The
looks on their faces showed there was no for-
giveness, no mercy, just cold, heartless fury.

"Ma'am." The deep voice startled her and
turned her around.

Charlotte, Dub, and Renny looked at a tall,
very handsome man in his late twenties or early
thirties. His hair was blond and very long, and
he sported a blond, heavily waxed handlebar
mustache.

The two outlaws couldn't believe the gall of
this tall stranger. He doffed his Stetson to
Charley, and she immediately felt confident that

her seemingly impossible problem was about to be solved.

The man said, "Name's Adams, ma'am, James Adams, at your service. Nobody was at the front desk, so I thought I'd see if you needed any help. It appears you do. Why don't you go back inside, while we parley out here?"

Dub pointed the gun at Adams and snarled, "She ain't goin' nowhere, sodbuster. And you ain't neither, 'cept to a early grave."

James Adams chuckled and said, "Sir, I assure you, I'm no farmer. I have a little freight line, and secondly, nobody is going to an early grave, except for you and your friend if you're still going to be unreasonable."

James Adams still held his hat in his hand, and he slowly moved it around in a circle with his hands on the brim.

Renny cocked his own Colt .45 and said, "Mister, ya shore kin talk some horse droppins' when we both got the drop on ya."

James smiled. "Last chance, gents, for you both to apologize to the young lady and leave."

Dub and Renny looked at each other and chuckled. They didn't notice James's right hand move from the brim and into the crown of the hat. There was a loud explosion as a hole suddenly appeared through the top of the Stetson, smoke and flames pouring through. At the same time, a large red hole appeared in the center of Dub's forehead, and the hat dropped, revealing the double-barreled .44 derringer in James's hand. Renny stared at the bottom barrel a split second before he saw the flames shoot out of it, and he saw the sky spin past his head, then felt the back of his head slam hard into the ground. The blood flooding into his open eyes kept him from seeing, and then he just stopped all thinking.

Charlotte's legs went weak and James Adams stepped forward to catch her up in his arms. She could feel the muscles through his tailored coat.

She looked up at him and said, "You saved my life, Mr. Adams. Thank you so very much."

He said, "It was nothing, ma'am. Now let's gather up your eggs, and I'll go find the marshal and make a report to him."

"No need to."

They turned to see the marshal coming down out of the back door of the hotel.

He said, "I saw it walking down the hallway. These two never should have come back to town. You don't even have to tell me the conversation. I can imagine."

Still stunned, Charlotte simply said, "This man saved my life, Marshal."

"That he did, Miss Colt, that he sure did."

James Adams had never tasted a breakfast like the one Charley Colt made for him that morning. He wanted to eat the entire cherry pie instead of the generous slice he was eating with a large glass of milk. He was already stuffed from the giant steak, home-fried potatoes, bread and butter, and three scrambled eggs he had eaten. She also made the best coffee he had tasted in months, and he had eaten in some of the finest hotels and restaurants in Denver, Cheyenne, Santa Fe, and many points east.

Two months later, another incident happened that was a turning point in their new relationship. James Adams had been seeing another woman for a long time, by the name of Elizabeth Greer Barrington. She lived in Santa Fe and was not very happy with it or the arid Southwest. She was born and raised in Philadelphia and dearly missed "civilization."

During the time he had now known Charlotte Colt, he had been a perfect gentleman and had really not shown any romantic interest, except in the way he looked at her. That, she could sense.

James had been to the town twice, as he had

short freight runs within New Mexico territory. The freight line he ran employed five employees and was very special. He drove a large freighter wagon loaded with anything of great value. One employee was a booker and shipper and worked out of Denver. James was principal driver with one man who was relief driver and the others were armed guards who escorted the wagon. He carried only freight that was very expensive and usually very fragile.

James's reputation was such that a person knew that they could move from Taos, New Mexico Territory, for example, to Montana and have their heirloom piano moved along with crystal candelabra, knowing that they would arrive in the same condition that they were in before shipping.

On the third trip to Cimarron since meeting Charley, he brought along his fiancée who wanted to visit an ill aunt in Trinidad, Colorado, just north of the border. Her aunt Grace was dying of consumption and had treated her well when Elizabeth was a child. Naturally, Elizabeth blamed the Wild West for her favorite aunt's impending death.

She had only been in Cimarron for a few hours and already she was tired of hearing about the "wonderful meal" they were going to have, prepared by such a great lady, Charlotte Colt. When she heard the name, Elizabeth felt her face redden and her ears actually burned. She was jealous, very jealous, but she was also angry at herself for being so.

Finally, the dreaded hour came, twelve noon; lunchtime. James met his fiancée in the hallway outside her room, held Elizabeth's arm, and escorted her downstairs to the dining room. There, he was cheerfully greeted by Charley who saw that his wagon and escort team were back in town. She did look a little perplexed when she saw Elizabeth, not knowing that James was engaged but hoping he was totally uninvolved. He reached out and took her hand.

"Miss Colt," he said, "How very good to see you again. I would like to introduce you to my fiancée, Miss Elizabeth Greer Barrington. Liz, this is Miss Colt, manager of this fine establishment, and she cooks some of the most marvelous meals you've ever tasted."

Charley felt a chill run through her when she heard the word "fiancée," and she felt like she wanted to cry without understanding why.

Elizabeth offered her hand to Charlotte, holding it like it was covered with filth.

She smiled sweetly, saying, "Well, we'll have to just see how good this cooking is. Won't we?"

Charlotte said, "I do hope you enjoy your meal, Miss Barrington."

Elizabeth couldn't help herself, "Well, I'm most outspoken, my dear; if I don't, I will let you know. When I pay good money for service or a product, I expect fair barter."

Charley gritted her teeth and smiled sweetly herself, replying, "I bet you do, Miss Barrington. You look like a woman of substance who enjoys the best and expects the best. That must be why you want to marry Mr. Adams."

James smiled and made a mock bow to Charley, but Elizabeth bristled, hiding it behind another phony smile. Charlotte definitely didn't like this woman, but she politely led the pair to a nice table near the window. She normally did not seat people and had plenty of fine help now, but she always wanted to seat and serve James Adams, who treated her so nicely.

Elizabeth brought this up, saying, "This is quite an honor being shown to our table by the hotel manager. Do you do this for all your guests?"

Charley said, "No, but not all of our guests saved my life like your fiancé did."

Elizabeth was shocked. She had not heard of this, and she stared at James.

"James," she said, "why haven't we spoken of this? How did you come to save her life?"

Charley was embarrassed, but secretly pleased.

James said, "Oh, it was nothing really, darling."

Charlotte enthusiastically replied, "Oh, but it was, Miss Barrington. He was absolutely heroic! Why two men were about to kill me, and Mr. Adams appeared from nowhere and intervened on my behalf. The men were definitely going to kill me, and I'm certain, worse. They planted both scoundrels in Boot Hill after Mr. Adams finished with them."

Elizabeth was white of face and without words. Finally, when the color started back into her face it came in floods of anger-red.

She looked at James, saying, "What were you doing, James, defending her honor?"

James said, "No, her life."

Charley was secretly loving this.

She added, "And I might add, he gave each of those black monsters a third eye."

Elizabeth looked at her and shuddered.

"How crude and vulgar," she finally exclaimed.

Charley chuckled and said, "Damned right!"

Elizabeth stood up and threw her chin in the air, saying, "Why, I never!"

Charlotte could not stand this woman when she saw her, and the more she put on airs and the more she talked, the more Charlotte disliked her.

Charley said, "And you probably never will."

Charlotte turned on her heel, grinning, and walked away. Out of the corner of her eye, she saw Elizabeth storm across the room and out the door. She also could not help but notice the slight grin trying to work its way at the corner of James Adams's mouth.

It was less than an hour later that Charley heard screams coming from Elizabeth's room. Elizabeth had a room on the first floor of the hotel, and it was just inside the hallway from the back door. During the hot evening the night before, a twelve rattle buzz tail had come out from under the shadows and slithered up the back stairs. He coiled up and lay under a rocking chair for an hour, then entered the building through a mouse hole that had been chewed into the wood the previous week. He found no meal in there so he worked his way into the room where Elizabeth stayed. It was a little cooler staying in the shaded area between several valises, so he had been there for some time now.

When Charley heard the screams, Elizabeth had gone to her room, deciding to change into a blue lamé and velvet dress. She thought about fetching James to lift her valise onto the bed for her, but then thought better of it. She figured he might think she was being a sissy and would compare her actions with what he would expect of that trashy hotel manager. Her face got beet-red thinking about it, and she literally felt her ears heat up as if they were near a flame.

Why would she even think of such a woman? she wondered. True, Charlotte was attractive in a low-class sort of way, she thought, but the hussy had nowhere near the background, schooling, and class as she.

Elizabeth reached across the first bag to lift the dress bag and it proved to be too heavy, so she moved around and stood in the corner of the room and lifted it and set it across the other one with the help of an uplifted knee. As soon as her foot touched the ground she heard the rattle and looked down next to the other valise. The rattlesnake was coiled up and ready to strike. That's when she started screaming.

Within a dozen seconds, James Adams and a nearby blacksmith, both appeared in the doorway. James immediately saw the problem and held up his hand, while the other hand searched for the gun that had been left back in his room. The blacksmith looked down at the heavy hammer in his hand and wondered how much it might help. Both men immediately knew that moving near the snake might make him strike, for he seemed to be getting angrier, or more scared by the second, depending on how you perceive buzz-tail behavior.

James said softly, "Elizabeth, you must stop moving and making noise. It will make him strike."

She screamed even louder hopping on both of her legs in total panic. The snake went backward to strike out hard and a loud explosion wiped out the buzzing and all sounds for both men. All they heard was ringing in their ears, and they saw the head of the rattler disappear in a splash of blood and matter. Elizabeth screamed even more and vibrated with her hands covering her face. The two men looked down at the smoking gun between them and back at Charley Colt, who had just accomplished the quick draw and very impressive shooting.

Both men turned their attention to Charlotte who calmly holstered her gun, but inside wanted to scream from the adrenaline rushing through her system. She was carrying the holster and gun belt in her hand.

The blacksmith said, "Dadgum, thet was shore some shootin', Miss Colt."

James said, "That's for sure. Miss Colt, where did you ever learn to handle a gun like that?"

Angrily, Elizabeth said, "Is anybody going to see if I am okay?"

The blacksmith said, "Ya ain't dead, is ya? The buzz tail's the one with problems."

James stepped over to her quickly and took her in his arms. She started sobbing as she lay her head against his chest.

He whispered, "Miss Colt saved your life. Aren't you going to thank her?"

Elizabeth stepped back, angry, and frustrated.

She said, "Thank you very much, Miss Colt, for shooting that awful thing."

Turning to James, she went on, "And now I suppose you'd like to go salivate all over her for her savage abilities."

This was the last straw. James didn't know it was until right then. All of a sudden, it hit him full in the face. His fiancée was a phony, conniving, shallow woman, and he had been fooling himself for a long time. On top of that, James realized all in one fell swoop that he was indeed in love but it was with Charlotte Colt.

He looked at Elizabeth and said, "Now that you mention it, I would love just that. Good-bye, Elizabeth."

He turned and walked from the room with both women staring after him, and the blacksmith grinning and nodding in approval.

Charley said to Elizabeth, "You better go get your man."

Elizabeth shrugged her shoulders and said, "Humph, I'll chase no man. Besides, he is set on us living out here in this blistering hell."

"Hell!" Charley said, "You call this hell? Why this is heaven and you don't even know it! The beauty of the sunsets with the reds and purples on the mountains there, the sound of bull elks whistling and grunting challenges to one another, and the steam coming off the backs of bison on a nippy fall morning, or the colors of a trout jumping out of the still waters of a pond at daybreak."

Neither woman saw James, who felt he had been too abrupt, as he returned and stood in the shadows of the doorway.

Elizabeth said, "If you love it here so much, why don't you go after him?"

Charley said, "Woman! What is wrong with you? That is your man! Why would you talk such drivel? It's women like you who make all of us look to men like sissified little church mouses, with no brains, no gumption, and no common sense. James is your man. You are crazy to let him slip away. You should go after him and apologize for embarrassing him."

Elizabeth said, "Sounds to me like you're the one who wants to marry him, not me."

Charley was furious now and her emotions did the speaking, "Well, if he was my man, I would never let a man like James Adams get away. I would fight anyone tooth and nail who tried to take him, but I don't go after men who are already taken. You should have that attitude."

Elizabeth said, "Well, I don't. I want to go back east."

James walked in the room and Elizabeth's face flushed, while Charley's heart skipped a beat again, and she realized she did indeed love him.

James said softly, "I believe that's a very good idea, Elizabeth. You do belong back there. I'm going to the depot now to buy a ticket on the train, one way, and you can go."

Now Elizabeth felt flustered and rejected. Not knowing what else to say, she said, "What about the wedding? You mean there will be no wedding?"

James said, "Yes, I'm sure you'll find some Eastern dandy who can give you what you want and you'll marry him and be happy. I wish that for you. As for me, I will have a wedding, but it will be with Charlotte."

Charley felt like she was going to faint. The words hit her in the pit of the stomach like a sledgehammer, but she also noticed she didn't protest or complain. Now, her heart started beating about two thousand beats a minute, and she wanted to skip around and sing. She felt more elation than at any time in her life.

CHAPTER 3

Big Brother

The valley that ran between Buena Vista and Salida, Colorado, was wide in some places, narrower in others, and most of it was covered with small hills covered with rocks and piñon trees. The Arkansas River began its headwaters up above the boomtown of Leadville, a town of 10,000-plus feet elevation. The headwaters came down in rivulets and streams wide enough to stand astraddle of running out from under dirty brown snow patches and shiny-topped frozen glaciers, all melting in the late spring or early summer sunshine. By the time the Arkansas dropped to Buena Vista there were sections of churning white-water rapids with water tearing through the narrow gorges at the speed of a hurricane and the force of a runaway train. In the meantime, at both sides of the valley stood majestic 14,000-plus-foot snowcapped peaks, tall, silent sentinels to the action and interaction down below caused by their melting glaciers.

The five hombres riding along the churning river had their eyes glued to the ground carefully watching the tracks of the big black-and-white paint gelding they followed.

Billy Rivera had been followed by the man after ignoring everyone's advice and traveling into Leadville anyway to spend some of the double eagles they had robbed off the mining company's wagon. The man on the big paint followed Billy right to their camp and took a bullet only by a mere fluke.

Billy was the offspring of a Mexican vaquero and a wealthy rancher's daughter in southern Texas. She had been raised and bred to marry into wealth and position and instead fell in love with a cowboy from Sonora. They had run off together when it was discovered she was carrying Billy. The couple was very much in love and was never given a minute's rest, as her father hired person after person to try to hunt them down and kill the father. After ten years, one of the bounty hunters shot Billy's father from ambush but couldn't stop at that. He figured, after all this time and trouble, he should kill Billy's mother, too. So he did and then was hunted down and hung himself by her father. This left Billy to raise himself and a mistrust for everyone, especially gringos. He was taken in by an outlaw gang and was on the owl-hoot trail immediately.

The Janover brothers were identical twins and both were double evil, double mean. Wearing bright shocks of tousled red hair, they had freckles all over their bodies, blond eyebrows, and blue eyes. The Janovers were poison-mean and had been that way since childhood. They would often get each other into gunfights as a personal joke with each other, but the fights were never with any skilled fighters. They were always against farmers, ranchers, merchants, drunks, anybody that didn't seem like he could win a gunfight.

Two years earlier, however, Brad Janover got an identifying mark that would distinguish him from his one-hour-older brother Mark. Trying to be funny, Mark picked a fight for his brother with a drunken cowhand in Abilene, not knowing that the man had been a former town marshal, then deputy sheriff, and had five confirmed kills in gunfights. Even though the puncher was dead drunk because of hearing about the loss of his sister to diphtheria, he still outdrew Brad and tore the redhead's cheek open with a .44 slug. Fortunately for Brad, the former lawman went down permanently with a bullet from a .44/.40 in his back courtesy of Mark.

Jimmy Joe Robb was a lanky youngster from the Cumberland Gap region who came out west because of wanderlust. He always seemed to be full of spunk and peewater growing up, they all said around home, and he journeyed to the great frontier to experience adventure. He had fallen in with this gang and now could not figure out how to leave them, alive at least. They intimidated him and his quest for adventure had taken on a dull sheen since joining up with these cutthroats. Jimmy Joe just wanted to go somewhere and join the cavalry and hunt for Geronimo or something, but he knew he was headed for hell in a hurry.

The leader of the gang was a spindly sort of man with a ratlike face and buckteeth. A former schoolteacher, Cedric Willow had been caught with a teenaged student in a compromising position back in Missouri by a prominent city councilman. He asked the man to have coffee with him before the man reported him, as he wanted to plead his case. Unfortunately, the councilman wasn't too terribly bright and trusted too much.

The coffee was laced with powerful poison

and Cedric Willow's criminal career had begun. As it had happened with other men cut from the same bolt of cloth, Cedric had never been in a fight before in his life, let alone never having won one. He enjoyed the power he felt by eliminating an enemy, so within a year, he hired out to a friend to kill the man's wife who had been unfaithful with a neighboring rancher. This time, he used a club on her and dumped her down a deserted mine shaft. He didn't have to chance poison this time, as she was much smaller than his own slight frame and wouldn't have weighed 100 pounds, soaking wet, holding a tub of churned butter. Killing her was exhilarating to him because she was taken down with force, albeit a club swung first in surprise from behind.

After that, he decided to move west and started practicing with a pistol every second he was awake. He dry-fired his pistols over and over again, while he rode his horse, while he walked to the store, while he did chores. He never stopped practicing until he became very fast with either hand.

After that, he challenged his first opponent to a gunfight, coincidentally in Abilene. He drew first on an inexperienced sixteen-year-old boy. They buried the lad.

After that, there were eleven others and nine did actually have guns.

Cedric Willow was now to the point where he was constantly looking for other men to fight to challenge his skills and conquer his nervousness. He loved the exhilaration afterward. As much as he hated the feelings of gastric pains, nausea, and shakiness before gunfights, he was addicted to it.

The former schoolteacher was so far removed from his previous life, it was like a rooster becoming a wolverine. He was now a cold, ruthless killer of men, who had no mercy or sympathy for anybody. Still a snip of a man in size, he certainly looked like anything except a killer, but that he was.

When the big man on the paint followed Rivera into camp and drew down on the gang, he didn't see Cedric Willow just happened to be returning from a "nature calls" trip into the trees. He had removed his gun belt and had not tied it back on, so his hand was actually on the butt of his right-hand .44. He fired with the gun still in the holster and the bullet took the big man through the back of his right side. If he would have turned to fire, the second or third bullet would have hit him before he spun around, but instead the man instinctively did a forward shoulder roll the split second after he was struck by the bullet.

He dashed into the trees on the far side of the camp holding his side while dodging from side to side with bullets raining all around him. Not long after he disappeared, the gang heard the whistle of a red-tailed hawk, followed by the drumming beat of fading away hoof falls.

While the man rode he ripped the red kerchief from his neck and tore it into two strips with his teeth. He tied these together and made one long bandage. Next he reached back into the loops on his gun belt and pulled out three cartridges. He placed these bullets together in the kerchief and wrapped it around one time. Next, he held the reins of the galloping horse in his teeth while he wrapped the bandage around his waist, the three bullets directly over the bullet hole in his side. He tied the kerchief off as tightly as he could and the three bullets created direct pressure on the bullet hole and this stopped the bleeding almost immediately.

He ran for a half mile, then slowed the big horse to alternate between a fast trot and a slow lope. He kept this up for a long time until the horse let him know he was getting winded and he slowed to a walk. This went quickly to a slow walk, then when the man felt the horse had been carefully cooled down, he dismounted and led the horse by the reins.

After a while he remounted and rode slowly for another ten miles before camping. Once during the journey, he climbed a tall knoll and saw the distant dust cloud of the gang chasing him. Wounded though like he was, he smiled. This man was a warrior, and he wanted them chasing him. Just a short ride above Buena Vista, he stopped the big paint alongside the roaring white-water Arkansas River. Getting fresh bandaging from his saddlebags he removed his shirt and temporary bandage, tossing the red cloth into the wet fury.

It was not necessary to explain this man to anybody if he would simply remove his buckskin shirt when he met people. His tanned and sinewy body painted a living portrait of his past. Through the right thigh was a bullet hole scar that entered the back and exited the front of the large thigh muscles. A more grotesque pair of entry/exit scars were found on the left shoulder near the collarbone. The bullet had entered the front and made just a small hole, but mushroomed while exiting the back and tore a large jagged hole there. There were two scars above the nipples on his massive pectoral muscles, where a shaman had pierced the flesh with eagle's talons and stuck two wooden pegs through. Leather thongs were attached to these while the man performed the sundance ceremony and pulled back with the thongs against the heavy buffalo skulls weighing them down after they had been passed over a pole in the ceiling of the sundance lodge. The man danced forward and back, staring up at the sun through the hole in the center of the lodge. He did this with the flesh on his chest being pulled out grotesquely, until the flesh finally tore away and the man fell in a faint having a vision.

On the right side of his abdomen low down was a knife scar and the little finger of his left hand had been cut off with a knife. There were three long claw marks, apparently from a bear or mountain lion, on his very large right bicep. There was also a minute, almost imperceptible, scar on one cheek from a razor-sharp arrow. It was only visible when the man smiled, which was often. His hazel-colored, very intelligent eyes, in fact, always seemed to be slightly smiling, as if he knew a secret that nobody else knew. His face was chiseled and ruggedly handsome, and he could have been in his late twenties or early thirties, but nobody really knew his age. His dark brown hair wasn't too long, and it pretty much traveled where it wanted. But, unlike that of some men, it added to his appearance.

He was tall, maybe six-four, and his body had shown he had been used to many years of hard work. His muscles were large and firm and his whole body was well-balanced.

He looked over at the big paint, a gift to him from Crazy Horse, his blood brother. The gelding still wore an eagle feather in his mane and one in his tail in tribute to his former owner, and he had three red coup stripes painted around each upper foreleg. The man had named the big mount, War Bonnet.

The man's name was Deputy U.S. Marshal Christopher Columbus Colt and he was one of the most famous trackers and gunfighters in the West. When men in saloons spoke of shootists, names came up like John Wesley Hardin, Clay Allison, Wyatt Earp, Doc Holliday, and others. Almost always included in that list was Chris Colt, Charlotte's brother, who didn't even know of her existence.

Chris Colt had indeed been tied up in the village of Crazy Horse in the great encampment at the Battle of the Greasy Grass, as the Sioux (Lakotah) and Cheyenne called it. It was better known as the Battle of the Little Big Horn. After that, he was a chief of scouts and ended up escorting the famous orator and chief of the Nez Perce called Chief Joseph on his famous 1,700-mile fighting retreat while being pursued by half of the U.S. Cavalry. It was the first time in American history where the press and the public actually became sympathetic to the Indian's side. He also helped the buffalo soldiers of the all-black Ninth and Tenth Cavalry in their campaign to hunt and bring down the Apache war chief Victorio.

Following this, Chris Colt became a Deputy U.S. Marshal and was now hunting down bad men all over Colorado and the surrounding territories and states.

In the case of these five, they had hit not only the payroll of a mining company but there was some government money in there as well. Because it was no easy trip to Leadville from anywhere, the government made a deal with one of the larger mining companies to carry the payroll for its assayers and other handful of employees who had moved to Leadville. The gang had hit the payroll and killed one and wounded two in the process. One of the bags contained freshly minted gold double eagles, and Colt who had gone to Leadville to investigate, was summoned when Billy Rivera showed up spending them on women and liquor.

The bullet had entered and exited the lower left side of Colt's kidney area but missed everything vital. It tore a hole through the left side abdominal muscle. Colt washed it along the banks of the churning river and poured whiskey through it. Then he cleaned it up with bandages. Colt hadn't lost much blood and he knew that the wound wasn't serious.

He ate a quick meal of hardtack and an apple, along with several mouthfuls of ice cold glacial river water. That was a better meal than many others he had eaten before while hunted.

He figured he had thirty minutes to half an hour before the others would catch up with him and that would give him time to prepare. Colt got the spare Bowie knife from his saddlebags and looked for some soft ground.

Billy Rivera rode point as kept his eyes on the large hoofprints running along the Arkansas. The other four followed in line with young

Jimmy Joe Robb taking up the rear of small column.

War Bonnet pranced in the trees where he was tied as he saw the other five horses walking slowly along the river. He whinnied because he was a horse, but they were too far away to hear. The roar of the river was loud in the ears of anything that passed by. He pranced and tried to shed the leather pads that felt so foreign to his hooves. Colt used them to sneak back and not leave more tracks.

Chris Colt felt the vibrations of the horses as they passed. It was dark and dank and he wanted to raise up and burst free, but he forced himself to remain patient. He held the reed in his mouth and tried to breathe slowly as he counted the horses walking by. One of the patches over his right eye had shifted to the left, and he felt dirt falling onto the eyelid.

What if they decided to stop here and camp, he thought, and then grinned at himself in the darkness. Not a good spot and way too early in the day, even for lazy outlaws.

He felt the vibrations of the fifth horse as it rode by. Jimmy Joe looked down at the droppings of the paint horse as he rode by the broken dead tree branch lying on the ground. He looked back at the backtrail and turned to the front wondering about the wounded man they followed. The branch moved and the droppings fell off to the side, as Chris Colt sat up, pushing the pile of carefully cut sod off to the side. He spit the reed from his mouth and removed the blanket that was covering him in his shallow self-made grave. Colt watched the back of the young man as he slowly walked away. He jumped out of the hole, his moccasins making no noise as he sprinted toward the rider and horse. Colt noticed the trail-wise horse glance back and see his approach, but the old steed was used to men and horses running around him and didn't shy much. Jimmy Joe noticed the horse's ears turn to the back and felt his muscles bunching up under him, so he turned his head to look back. He was too late, however, as Chris Colt vaulted over the horse's rump and landed behind the young man. His left hand went around the teenager's mouth and his Bowie knife's blade almost cut into Jimmy Joe's windpipe.

Colt whispered, "Don't breathe or you'll have a new mouth. Just ease back on the reins."

Jimmy Joe wanted to nod his head affirmatively but was afraid to even swallow. He watched his riding partners and his hopes ride out of sight around the bend in the river. Colt whispered, "All right, turn him around and take me back to my blanket." They rode up to Colt's hiding place and Jimmy Joe gulped as he realized the man had been that close to him as he passed seconds before.

Colt sheathed his knife and drew one of his six guns. He hopped down and rolled up his blanket. Jimmy Joe slowly reached down for his pistol and was surprised that his holster was empty.

Without looking up, Colt said quietly, "I hope you don't think I'm that dumb, youngster."

Colt pulled the boy's gun out of his gun belt and showed it to him. Jimmy Joe's heart sank even deeper.

Chris stuck his foot in the stirrup, after handing the young man the rolled-up blanket, and he swung up behind him again, jamming the gun barrel in Jimmy Joe's ribs.

Colt said, "Over there into those trees."

The outlaw touched his heels to the bay's ribs, and they trotted to a small hillock covered with trees. Riding up into the trees, they came upon War Bonnet who whinnied at the strange horse. The bay whinnied back. Chris slid off the horse's rump and walked over to War Bonnet who nuzzled his friend, placing the blanket behind the saddle and tying it in place. Chris then pulled a pair of manacles from his saddlebags and motioned for Jimmy Joe to dismount. Colt cuffed the young man to a tree and tied the bay horse to another.

He then jumped in his own saddle and grabbed a lariat that was attached to a large branch. He took two wraps around his saddle horn and rode out to the spot where he had hidden. Chris jumped down, replaced the sod, dragged the branch over the tracks, and returned back to the trees. Next, he tied the rope onto a bushy pine branch and rode back over the same ground dragging the thick branch. Dust swirled around as he again wiped out all evidence of his trail with the pine branch.

Watching all this from the distance, Jimmy Joe was amazed at the thoroughness, as Chris jumped down and ran back to the spot, jumping from rock to bush clump to hide his own footprints. He arrived at his former hiding spot and worked his way back, on foot, picking up pine needles that came loose from the branch.

No sooner had Colt made it back into the trees than the other four outlaws came into view looking for Jimmy Joe Robb. They arrived at the end of the tracks and eventually dismounted, Cedric even dropping to his knees to look for tracks. Colt chuckled as he saw that one found something by the river and motioned for the others to come over. Apparently, they figured the kid had deserted them and attempted to go into the killer river. They looked at the rapids and seemed totally lost, finally mounting up, and riding on.

Colt went over to Jimmy Joe and uncuffed him from the tree. He then cuffed the lad's hands behind his back and motioned him into a bowl near the top of the hill.

Chris said, "We'll have something to eat and a few hours' sleep. I'm going to be busy tonight. By the way, you're under arrest."

Jimmy Joe said, "Good, I'm glad to be plumb outta thet truck. Thet Cedric Willow is one crazy hombre and the rest ain't fer behind, sir. Marshal, kin I ast what yer name is?"

Colt said, "Colt. Chris Colt."

Jimmy Joe's eyes opened wide.

He exclaimed, "Yer Chris Colt! And them boys shot ya? Oh, man, am I lucky ta be alive. I cain't believe ya ain't skint me inside out."

Colt grinned and said, "I still might if you don't behave."

Colt built a smokeless fire with dry wood and let the trees filter the smoke out. The outlaws were gone around the bend in the river and the valley and would not be able to see the smoke anyway. After dark, the natural bowl they were in would prevent any eyes from spotting the fire.

He carved off some slices of bacon, fried wild turnips, and made biscuits as well. He also made some fried apple and a big pot of coffee. Jimmy Joe ate heartily and confessed that he hadn't eaten so well in a coon's age.

Colt said, "Thought you and your compatriots got plenty of gold in the heist."

Jimmy Joe said, "Cedric controls all that and won't let nobody near it since Billy went back to Leadville and spent some. Cedric took everyone's money back and said he'd hold it till things cooled off. I was glad anyhow, 'cause I ain't cut out fer this outlaw stuff. I don't like none a them a whit, an I wasn't involved in the holdup anyhow. They made me keep the camp and tend to the extry horses, but I got a cut a the money an ain't blind, so's I ain't tryin to worm outta what I done."

"If you don't like them, why didn't you leave them?"

Jimmy Joe cleared his throat and said, "Hate to admit it, sir, but I was scaret a Cedric. He's about the coolest, meanest gent I ever seed."

Colt took a sip of coffee and lit a cigarette. He offered the makings to the boy, who rolled a cigarette, his hands having been freed to eat.

Colt said, "Why you hanging out with that crowd anyway, boy?"

Jimmy Joe said, "Wal, Mr. Colt, I come out west a ways back 'cause I was always pokin' mah nose in where they was trouble. I throwed in with them characters and have been plumb sorry fer it ever since. I wished I weren't so dang dumb."

Chris smiled and fed sticks into the fire. He looked at a far-off snowcapped peak and blew smoke at it.

Colt said, "Son, there was a young man about your age who once came up to a giant ranch house out on the prairie. The ranch was surrounded by several large stock ponds and some of the longest greenest grass you ever saw. There were big fat cattle everywhere and the ranch house had several barns and two bunkhouses. The remuda was collected in several corrals and were some of the best put-together horses you ever saw. There was an old man sitting in a rocking chair on the porch smoking a pipe and looking out over all his holdings."

Colt paused for dramatic effect and took a

long drag on his cigarette and poured more coffee for himself and the younger man. He sipped on the coffee, as Jimmy Joe leaned forward in anticipation of the rest of the story.

Colt went on, "It was obvious, even by the man's clothes or the crystal glass of sherry he was holding that he was extremely wealthy and successful.

"The young cowpuncher said to the old man, 'Sir, I beg your pardon but can you tell me how a man can make himself an empire like this for himself?'

"The old man took a pull on his pipe and said, 'Wise decisions.'

"Then the young cowboy said, 'But, sir, how do you learn how to make wise decisions like that?'

"The old man took another long pull on his pipe and looked at the kid and simply said, 'Experience.'

"The cowboy said, 'Experience? But, sir, how can you get that kind of experience?' "

Colt took another couple of drags on his cigarette and carefully put it out, tearing the butt apart between his thumb and index finger and letting the tobacco and paper be carried off by the wind.

Colt said, "The old man leaned forward and answered the kid, 'Foolish decisions.' "

Chris leaned back against the tree and drank his coffee.

Jimmy Joe said, "Huh?"

The young man thought about the story for a few minutes and the gist of it finally hit him full in the face. He would get through this, he decided, somehow and pay his jail time or whatever he had to do and never run afoul of the law again.

By now, Colt had rolled out his bedroll and used his saddle as a pillow. It was as if he could read the boy's mind. Colt tossed the kid his pistol and the young man was astounded.

Jimmy Joe said, "What's this for, Marshal Colt?"

Chris said, "I hear the weather's good up in Wyoming and Montana both right now and a lot of spreads are looking for young hands that will work to earn an honest-day's wages."

The boy got tears in his eyes and wiped them away.

Colt said, "If you disappoint me, son, and take the path again, and I figure you've decided to leave, I'll hunt you down and kill you."

Jimmy Joe said firmly, "Mister Colt, you'll

never have to worry about thet. I ain't ever gonna do nothin' but work hard and honest the rest a mah days. I figgered ef'n I'd have ta do time, I'd do it standin' up, then git out an walk the straight and narrow. I'll never fergit ya, sir. Never."

Colt said, "Well, good luck to you, partner. Remember the hardest way is usually the right answer."

Jimmy Joe grabbed his saddle and walked over to his horse and saddled him. He returned to Chris and shook hands with him.

He said, "Marshal, them boys was only gonna trail ya as long as ya headed long sides the Arkansas. Cedric wants ta hit the bank in Canon City."

Colt said, "Thanks, which bank?"

Jimmy Joe said, "Ah, it was Fremont County Bank."

Colt said, "Big mistake. That's where I keep my money. You can ride or you can rest here first. Your choice."

Jimmy Joe said, "Marshal Colt, I'm gonna head north as fast as this here horse kin carry me. Well, see ya."

"Keep a close eye to yer backtrail, son," Colt

said, smiling, "but spend most of your time concentrating on the trail that lies ahead of you."

Colt lay in his bedroll smiling to himself as he watched the young man ride out of sight. When the lad turned to wave a final good-bye, Chris just pretended like he was asleep. He hated saying good-bye to anybody, and he felt good about the kid. Letting Jimmy Joe go was a good decision, Colt decided. He thought the kid would do all right for himself, and Chris thought about the various people who gave him breaks in his life. Like the Confederate sergeant who spotted him hiding in a poison ivy patch in the Civil War. It was right in the midst of the enemy position and they were searching all around for the teenaged scout and infiltrator. The war was almost over. The unit was ready to move out. Maybe the sergeant had a son like him at Colt's age. He walked over to where Chris was hiding to relieve his bladder and spotted the young Union soldier and never gave him away.

That was the foremost example Chris Colt could think of of someone giving him a break in his life.

The other significant time came after the war. Chris Colt had returned to northeastern Ohio then, and soon after headed out west. When he arrived in Wyoming Territory in the town of Cheyenne, he went to the first saloon he could find, because he figured that was what young men were supposed to do out west.

Chris ordered a beer and heard chuckles in the saloon. The bartender handed him one with a wink and young Colt walked over to a table in the corner and sat down. He had already started a habit then after his frightening experiences in the war. Chris never sat down in a room without having his back to the corner, or wall, and facing the door. He just couldn't have it any other way. He felt too vulnerable.

He took his first sip of his first beer, and it tasted good to him after a hard day of riding in the hot July sunshine. He heard chuckles again and noticed a group of four cavalry troopers, three young privates, and one gray-haired corporal, sitting at a far table and laughing while making jokes among one another. They had about a fourth of a bottle of whiskey in front of them and each drank from a shot glass. Colt had the feeling by their mannerisms that the bottle wasn't their first one. Chris looked away and drank his beer, trying to push down the anger that was rising up in him now.

Finally, one of the privates could hold off no

longer and said, "Hey, Junior, don't ya need a nipple on top a thet glass?"

Chris tried to ignore the remark and the outright laughter going on now. He kept sipping his beer and finally decided he ought to leave and avoid the fight that he knew was coming. He had just finished fighting in a war and saw way too much action, especially for a young teenaged boy who had lied about his age to fight. He had no fear at all of the four troopers, except that he might go off half-cocked and kill somebody if he lost his temper.

Colt got up and walked toward the door, which took him past their table. The troopers laughed even harder as he focused his eyes straight ahead on the door, but the young veteran was just about at the limit of his patience. As he passed their table, the closest trooper stuck his foot out, but Colt was ready. Instead of tripping over it like most people would have done, he raised his foot and stomped down on the top of the other man's foot breaking several of the bones.

Colt walked out the door, hearing nary a peep, but it was only seconds before the remaining troopers worked up their whiskey-courage to go after the single man. They poured out the bat-wing doors behind him and Chris turned on the boardwalk to face them.

Suddenly, the old corporal saw something in Chris Colt's eyes that he had seen only once or twice over the years.

He grabbed one of the troopers by the arms and whispered, "C'mon, boys, let's forget it. We've had our fun."

The trooper pulled away and snapped at the corporal, "What's yer problem, O'Hare? He broke Del's foot, so we're gonna break some a his bones."

The old corporal said, "No, you ain't, boys. He's a warrior. I see it in his eyes. Don't crowd him no more."

The trooper said, "Bull, he ain't no warrior. He's a dad-blasted kid."

Christ Colt was mad, killing mad. He walked up face to face with the trooper, with their noses scant inches apart. His lips curled back over his teeth, Colt drew his Colt .44 Russian and cocked it with the end of his barrel against the trooper's belly. The color drained from the man's face.

Chris then whispered in a snarl, "Draw your gun, trooper."

Shaking, the trooper replied, "I cain't. Ya got the drop on me."

Colt said, "Draw it now or die."

The trooper, carefully, slowly drew his revolver from his flap-over holster. His hand was visibly shaking.

Colt now said, "Now, stick the end of your barrel against my gut, like I've done."

The man started to protest but Colt jabbed him with his own barrel. The trooper complied.

Colt then sneered, "Cock it."

The man couldn't believe this and replied, "What?"

Colt said, "You heard me. Cock it."

The trooper was sweating bullets now, but he cocked the gun and wondered what Colt would order next.

Chris said, "Now, let's both step back three paces."

The trooper breathed a little sigh of relief, not having the gun barrel against his belly, but he wasn't too comfortable as it was only seven or eight feet away now.

Chris Colt said, "Now, your corporal there is going to count three, and we pull the triggers. Bad shot loses. I figure you'll wound me 'cause you're so shaky, but I will darn sure kill you. You wanted a fight. You got one. Now, Corporal, you count or I'll pull the trigger anyway."

The corporal had no choice, so he said, "One."

The trooper, almost crying and in total panic, yelled, "Wait!"

The corporal said, "Two."

The trooper whimpered and dropped his pistol on the boardwalk as if it were made of hot fire embers.

Colt said calmly, "What's wrong, hardcase? Afraid to die? I'm not."

The trooper, a little braver now, feeling he wouldn't get shot if unarmed, said, "That's because you wanted us both to shoot point-blank. We both would get killed."

Working up his courage, he said, "I bet you wouldn't be so tough without a gun in your hand."

Without a word, Chris Colt tossed his .44 to the surprised corporal and Colt punched the trooper with a straight hard right. The punch landed on the point of the man's chin, and he fell butt-over-teakettles over the hitching rail. He started to his feet but lunged head-first into Colt's legs tackling the young man. Chris grabbed the man from above in a bear hug and lifted him upside down and dropped him on the boardwalk.

The bigger man jumped up, shook his head,

and lunged at Colt, his arms outstretched hoping to catch Colt in a tackle. Chris sidestepped and grabbed the back of the soldier's tunic as he passed and swung him, letting the man's centrifugal force and Colt's slight redirection send the man crashing face-first into the porch support for the second-floor porch.

Blood spurted everywhere from the man's mouth and nose, as he slid unconscious to the boardwalk.

Colt looked at the remaining troopers and said, "Looks to me, you boys are a lot better drinkers and talkers than fighters. Any more takers?"

They were all ashamed and glanced sheepishly at one another.

The corporal stepped forward and handed Chris his gun, saying, "Mister, you ain't no pilgrim and out here a man is a man by his actions, not his years. Yer one ta ride the river with. I been drinkin' and have a big mouth. Ya got my apology."

Colt smiled and simply nodded his head.

The trooper said, "I think I'll be hearing more of you. Mind if I ask your name?"

Chris said, "Colt," then turned and walked to his horse.

When he was almost there Colt heard what sounded like a lightning bolt hitting a tree next to him and realized a bullet had just gone by his ear. He dived forward drawing his gun while doing a somersault. Colt came up into a crouch just beyond a second bullet kicking up dust under his legs. He was killing mad, when he came up into a squatting position facing the shooter.

The trooper he had just beaten was holding his smoking revolver and his eyes opened wide as he tossed the gun down and started to raise his hands, but Chris fired three fast shots that literally exploded the trooper's chest.

One of the other troopers pointed and said, "Marshal, deed you see zat? Zee man was unarmed and raiseeng hees hands, *n'est-ce pas*?"

Colt turned to see the town marshal, a large, red-faced man with a big salt-and-pepper-colored walrus mustache, as he quickly approached Colt from behind.

The French-born trooper went on, "Marshal, are you goeeng to arrest zees killere?"

The marshal said, "No, I ain't, Froggie. I seen the shootin'. It was righteous. Now git for ah run ya in."

He walked up to Chris and grinned into the

young man's face. The French trooper started to speak but was grabbed by the upper arm by the old corporal and escorted away.

"Young 'un," the old lawman said, turning his attention to Chris. "If'n ya was a normal cowhand, ya'd already be swingin' from a rope. Now git fore ah change mah mind. Thet men had dropped his iron and was surrenderin' ya kilt 'im."

Chris said, "Thank you, Marshal, but why didn't you charge me?"

The marshal said, "Ya jist got back from the war, didn't ya, kid?"

Colt said, "How do you know?"

The marshal said, "Ya got the look. I lost mah boy in the war. He run off and enlisted an probably was yer age. Went down a man, though, at Bull Run."

Colt said, "A lot of good men went down in that war, Marshal. Sorry about your boy."

The marshal cleared his throat and said, "Damned dry dust. Git outta here, son."

Colt stuck out his hand and shook with the old lawman and went immediately to his horse and left without looking back. The killing would haunt him the rest of his days.

These two old men always remained in Colt's

memories, along with a pledge by him to never become out of touch so much with his own humanity, that he would forget human charity. He thought of the young man now departing and smiled, self-satisfied.

It was midnight when Chris Colt mounted up and took off along the white water. It was bright out with a full moon and the sky looking like God had spread a black velvet tablecloth over everything and covered the cloth with millions of diamonds. The ruts of the wagon road were clear and the water alone was dropping so rapidly in elevation that there was seldom a place that he could not be guided by the sound alone of the river, so much in a hurry to help the farmers and ranchers miles below out on the plains.

War Bonnet ate up the road, all slowly and unnoticeably downhill at a brisk trot. Occasionally, the big horse would break into a canter and Colt would let him go. Then he'd settle back into a trot, but it was one that other horses would have to lope to keep up with. It was miles down the road when he finally spotted what he was looking for, a faint red glow in the shadows. A small side gulch ran down to the river and someone was camped back in the trees, away from the road, away from the river.

Colt dismounted, switched to Lakotah soft-soled moccasins from his saddlebags, and left his horse where he was. There was immediate graze along the road and the horse would go no farther than five feet from where Colt ground-reined him.

Crazy Horse had taught the horse to ground tie a year before he gifted Chris Colt with the paint. He had a war bridle on the horse and buried a section of log in the ground where the tribe's bermuda grazed. There was a short rawhide-braided rope tied around the log, and it stuck out of the ground. Crazy Horse would ride up, dismount, and immediately wrap the rope into the bottom of the war bridle and make a slip knot. Learning he could not move from there, the horse eventually learned to stay where he was tethered and the lifelong habit was formed. All Colt had to do was drop the reins and that was where the horse would stay.

He went into the trees just north of the gulch and made his way quietly, stealthily through the stunted evergreens. The piñons and cedars were scattered at best and he made his way by moving slowly in the moon shadows, then dashed behind the growths where the trees grew close. Colt had hunted too many animals and men to be foolish enough to move quickly in the open. Moving slowly, almost imperceptibly, he knew he did not attract anywhere near the attention.

Chris made his way up to the top of the near ridge and slowly crawled over and down behind a thick cedar. Still crawling head-first, he carefully made his way down the slope, slowly, silently, removing each stick or rock in his path with his fingers. No stones rolled down the hill; no twigs cracked.

Soon, he was just outside the light of the dying embers. This time, he would not rush in without seeing that each man was in his bedroll. They were all there and all snoring. His stomach ached from his wound, but he stayed on his belly, propelling himself forward on his forearms and knees.

Chris really didn't have a plan right now, except that he hoped that Cedric Willow would make a play for a gun so he could repay him for the hole in his side. He was a lawman, so he wouldn't force a shootout, but he wished that he could.

When he was angry, Chris became a bit of a show-off, so he made his way right up to the campfire and dusted off his clothes, sitting on a log. He fed sticks into the fire until it was blazing. He got into the outlaws' supplies and made a large pot of black coffee and waited for it to boil. When it got hot, he rinsed out a metal cup and poured a steaming cup.

Brad Janover started to stir and opened his eyes, when his senses told him that there was coffee brewing. He sat up and looked right at Colt, then lay back and went right back to sleep. Suddenly, he sat bolt upright and stared at a grinning Chris Colt, who was holding a smaller Colt in his right hand, while sipping coffee from the cup in his left. Janover shivered and held his hands straight up in the air, looking around, as Chris gave him a shushing gesture. Colt nodded with his head, and the single twin tossed his guns forward to the fire. The gun belt had been draped over a forked stick stuck into the ground next to the outlaw.

Colt said, "Sure is good coffee, boys."

Mark Janover, with no surprise to his twin, kept snoring, but Cedric Willow immediately rolled to his left and came out of his blanket growling and cocking a Navy .36 he had hidden under his blanket. Colt fell backward off his log perch as the bullet spit past his face, his right-hand gun blossoming flame.

Mark came wide awake clawing for his .44s, but Colt's guns fired simultaneously hitting both men in the right shoulders. Both men dropped their guns screaming and Chris Colt was not ever going to let anyone, except maybe his brother Joshua know, that he had been aiming at the bulk of their bodies, not their shoulders.

Brad thought seriously about diving and rolling up with his Spencer carbine, but a warning smile from Chris changed his mind.

Taking advantage of the strange coincidence of his shooting, Colt said, "Now, now. You just saw me shoot two men in their gun hand shoulders at the same time in two different directions. Now the question you have to ask yourself is this: Am I really that dumb? Should I try for the rifle or take a chance with the judge in Canon City?"

Brad said, "We put a hole in ya. How do Ah know, ya ain't gonna put one in me, too? Ya plugged them."

Colt said coolly, "You don't know. Wanna try for it?"

Janover said, "No. Kin Ah tend ta my brother?"

Colt said, "No, you can't. I'll take care of him. You wrap your arms around that tree."

Colt pulled the coiled braided leather riata from his neck and tied the man to a tree, after removing the other men's guns from their reach. He then bound Willow's arms to his sides with Mark Janover's saddle rope, while he treated the twin's wounds. Next, he untied Cedric Willow and treated his shoulder. He then bound up the wounded Janover with the rope and tied Willow with the man's own lasso.

Leading the men tied over their saddles and with their wrists tied together under the horses' chests, he led his little train into Salida, along the Arkansas shortly after daybreak. Colt turned them over to the marshal who saw to their accommodations. The doctor arrived to tend to the wounds and that's when Brad, the unwounded twin, told the story about the simultaneous shootings and another Chris Colt story was born. As usual, it would be retold dozens of times in homes, stores, saloons, and bunkhouses over the next several years, except Chris would get a foot taller with each retelling of the story.

He left the marshal's office and walked down the street, looking for a nice meal. War Bonnet was being tended to at the livery and Colt paid extra for extra-special care. He decided that was something he could use himself. Spotting a friendly looking little restaurant, Colt walked in and the atmosphere reminded him of his first meeting with his wife, Shirley, who was then Shirley Ebert. It was in North Dakota Territory and the lovely woman owned a very successful restaurant, which she gave up to marry Chris Colt. She was a wonderful cook and tough-minded herself. Shirley had turned out to be a whole lot more than a wife or mother. She totally complemented Chris Colt in her own strengths and weaknesses, the former greatly outweighing the latter. The layout of this cafe reminded Chris so much of Shirley's former cafe, that he watched the kitchen doorway in anticipation, then laughed at himself as a large burly man in a dirty apron walked out.

Colt noticed trouble brewing before he even ordered breakfast. He recognized the big, rugged-looking hombre in the corner, his back to the wall, like Chris in the opposite corner. The man was all sand with plenty of bottom to him and had helped Chris and his Nez Perce sidekick out of a shooting scrape in New Mexico a few years earlier. Colt figured the man had spotted him before he even came through the door. Like Colt, he was the type that would have spotted and assessed everyone before he himself was noticed.

The trouble was brewing between the one man and two toughs that were dressed "south Texas." Colt stayed back and kept his nose out of it. The one young puncher had three notches on the butt of each of his tied-down .44s. It was the sign of a dude, or at least, want-to-be gunslinger. The two apparently had the remnants of last night's drunk still affecting them. If Colt was called on, he would intervene, but unless the opportunity presented itself the big man would resent the intrusion.

The two kept looking over at him and whispering jokes to each other and laughing. Colt just watched with interest. Chris was getting tired of it himself, but the good-looking, quiet man acted as if he hadn't heard a word. He had, though. As the laughing and giggling got louder and derogatory words became easier to hear, the man got up and headed for the door. Although he knew Colt, this was a time to walk away and not stop and chitchat. He knew it, and Chris knew it. On top of that, the man didn't want to involve Colt in his troubles. It wasn't his way. He just glanced sidelong at Chris as he passed near his

table and gave him a wink and almost imperceptible smile.

Chris was glad that an incident wouldn't happen, when the man just got his hand on the door-
knob and one of the punchers said, "Leavin'
'cause he's a yellow coward."

The man's hand stopped, and he turned. The
look he gave the punchers wiped the smile off of
both their faces. The speaker suddenly wished he
was somewhere else.

The big man didn't get into a gunfighter's
crouch. Anybody with experience could tell he
was relaxed but ready. His left hand hovered
cross-body near his belly gun, and his right was
just over his holster gun. As relaxed as he
looked, Colt knew he was like a coil spring,
ready to pop.

The big man said softly, "You can apologize for
that remark. You can leave. Your partner made
the remark."

The other man said, "I don't carry, Mister. He's
my ridin' partner. What he says goes fer me."

The quiet man said, "It's a free country."

Colt had enough. He was sick of the men he
had just brought in and was taking down to
Canon City. He was tired of all the so-called
hardcases that couldn't find their naked tails in a

darkened outhouse, using both hands. He chuckled out loud as the two would-be toughs got into a gunfighter's crouch. He stood up.

Colt said, "Boys, before you draw. I just want to introduce you to my friend here. You may have heard of him. His name is Sackett."

The two men had their eyes open wide, which they probably didn't really want to show. It happened anyway.

The speaker said nervously, "Mr. Sackett, Ah'm sorry. I drunk too much last night, and I got a big mouth."

Sackett said quietly, "Yes, you sure do, Mister. See you, Marshal Colt."

The speaker looked at Chris and repeated, "Colt?"

His eyes opened even wider, but his partner was the one who showed the real nerves, as he started to vomit and ran out the door and into the alley. Grinning, Colt watched the broad back of Sackett as he walked away, mounted his horse, and rode off. They would run into each other again somewhere and laugh about this story over a cold beer.

The next morning, Colt booked passage for himself and the three outlaws on the train heading down to Canon City. They had to stop for a herd of bighorn sheep covering the tracks while watering at the Arkansas River a few miles south of Cotopaxi. Chris wanted to unload his horse off the boxcar and ride the few hours home, but he had a job to do.

They reached Canon City by midafternoon, and Colt took the prisoners to the Fremont County jail. The doctor was summoned to administer to their wounds, and he finally, after some arguing and cajoling, worked on Colt, too.

Chris decided to spend the night in Canon City and soak in the mineral baths across from Old Max, the state penitentiary.

It was just after daybreak when Buzz Cooney rapped on Colt's hotel room door at the mineral baths. Chris Colt, wearing nothing but a double holster rig around his bare buttocks, answered the door, Colt Peacemaker in his right hand. When he saw it was a deputy sheriff, he holstered the gun and led the deputy into the room, opening the blinds. Colt splashed water on his face and smiled at the deputy, while slipping on his clothes.

"What do you need, Buzz?"

Buzz Cooney replied, "Sheriff wants to know if you can help us with a problem right quick, Mr. Colt?"

Chris said, "What kind of problem?"

Buzz responded. "You know old Bryce Stick Legs Betterton?"

"The drunk," Colt said. "Yeah, I know him."

Cooney said, "He beat his old lady again last night, and he's holed up in his cabin with a gun to her haid, swearin' we win't a gonna take him alive, or her, too fer that matter. His neighbor sent fer us when she heard the commotion an hour ago."

Chris strapped on his guns and headed for the door, "Come on. We better get there in a hurry."

Colt and Cooney rode up, an hour later, to a small cabin not far from the town of Beaver just east of the mouth of Phantom Canyon. The Fremont County sheriff was behind a very large cottonwood tree some distance from the cabin. A big grin spread across his large ruddy cheeks when he saw Colt riding up. Colt touched his hat and smiled. He knew he would be in for some teasing from the sheriff. He always was.

Colt sat his horse and said, "You wanted me, Ben?"

Just then a shot rang out from the cabin, and eyes opened wide, Cooney literally dived from his horse and sprinted for the cover of the tree, but Colt just sat on War Bonnet, grinning at the sheriff, his forearms crossed over the saddle horn. A little puff of a dust cloud still hung in the air fifty paces toward the cabin where the bullet spit up dust.

Colt said, "Deputy, he's shooting a pistol, and we're out of range."

Cooney said, "But, Marshal Colt, there's some bullets around that don't know how to act right."

Chris rode over to the cottonwood and dismounted.

The sheriff said, "Figured before you headed for home, you'd like to come out here to Beaver Creek and have a nice picnic lunch under the cottonwoods, Chris."

Colt pulled out a cigar and passed one to Cooney and the sheriff, lighting all three.

He took a long puff and said, "Oh, yeah. You've seen my wife and how pretty she is. I'd much rather be out here on a picnic with you, too, than to go home and kiss her and play with my children. I also like to go to Geronimo anytime I need a haircut."

The three chuckled, then the sheriff said, "Wal, you know ole Bryce Stick Legs Betterton. That's him in there tryin' to open ya up. He's got a gun on his wife and says he's gonna do her this time, along with himself, of course. Ya got his guns from him once before, so I sent Cooney here to fetch ya. Can ya figger somethin' out, Colt?"

They all turned their heads at the sound of hoofbeats and saw a handsome Indian dashing toward them on a large black Appaloosa horse with a white spotted rump and four white stockings. Alongside ran a 200-pound gray timberwolf, Colt's wolf Kuli. The young Nez Perce on the horse, Man Killer, did not have to work for Chris Colt as a deputy. He was married to the former Jennifer Banta of Westcliffe, who inherited a multimillion-dollar fortune, and he had all the money in the world he would ever need. On top of that, he was a ten percent shareholder of Colt's big Coyote Run ranch and was one of the premiere Appaloosa horse breeders in the country. His seed herd and stallions came directly from the herd of Chief Joseph, Man Killer's former chief and mentor. Chris Colt took Joseph's place as a mentor, some years before, while Man Killer was a teenager.

Colt looked over at the sheriff and said, "I have an idea."

Man Killer jumped off his horse before it had finished sliding to a stop, as bullets came from the cabin window, while Betterton yelled, "Take thet ya durned blanket-nigger!"

Petting Kuli vigorously, Colt said, "Old Stick Legs is nipping the juice again. What brings you here hell-bent-for-leather?"

Man Killer said, "We must go. They sent a wire for you, a killing in Denver."

Colt said, "They want me to go to Denver for a murder?"

Man Killer said, "Sheriff Schoolfield, rode to my ranch himself to bring the wire. He said that it is an important case."

Colt said, "Well, first let's see what I can do with Stick Legs Betterton."

Chris Colt called Kuli and took off running away from the cottonwood at right angles to the cabin. One shot came from the cabin but that was all. Chris ran out to the left until he was in a position where Bryce Betterton could not look out of either window or the door and see his approach.

Left-hand Colt out, he scampered toward the corner of the cabin and soon made it to the wooden porch, Kuli close at his heels. Colt crawled on his hands and knees and Kuli crawled behind him, as they made their way across the porch. The boards squeaked as they crawled.

Betterton's voice yelled through the open window, "I hear ya, Colt, dammit. Ya think yer a damned redskin, but I hear ya and ya ain't takin' me, Colt. You pop in that door or window and my ol' lady is gonna take a bullet betwixt the eyes. Ya heah?"

Chris stood up next to the door and yelled, "Betterton, either you come out with your hands up before I count to ten, or I'm sending my wolf in after you!"

Bryce yelled, "Ya better not send no damned wolf! Ya heah me, Colt? I ain't scaret anyhows!"

Chris leaned against the wall, cupping his mouth close to the door and made a series of loud vicious barks and growls.

Behind the large tree, Man Killer started laughing, saying, "Wolves do not bark. They only howl."

Nevertheless, Chris Colt stood by the front door growling and barking over and over again.

He said, "All right, I'm sending him in the door."

There was a crash of glass behind Chris and he wheeled both hands filled with Colt .45s. A pistol had crashed through the window and landed on the dirt just off the porch. A second crash followed and a shotgun flew out into the dirt.

From inside, Bryce yelled, "Hold on ta him,

Colt. Ah'ma comin' out with mah hands helt high. You heah? Holt on ta thet wolf."

Chris said, "I've got him. Come on out! No funny business!"

The door opened and the woman, one eye swollen shut walked out the door, Chris quickly grabbed her and pulled her behind him.

Stick Legs walked out next, with both long thin legs shaking like a bear cub was balancing at the top of each in a stiff breeze. Kuli walked over from behind Chris and gave the frightened man a big lick along the back of his hand.

Bryce looked over at Colt, and Chris grinning, growled and said, "Woof!"

Man Killer fell on the ground holding his stomach laughing and the sheriff had to hold the tree to keep from doing the same. The deputy, in the meantime, ran to the cabin carrying cuffs and leg irons, which he immediately placed on Bryce Stick Legs Betterton. By now, the old drunk was cursing everybody and everything in sight, including Colt and his wolf. The latter of which was the target of a would-be kick, which never occurred because of the leg irons. Bryce, however, did manage to land solidly and unceremoniously on his derriere. The cussing continued.

* * *

Johnny Ferrucio was a Pinkerton man who had been born and raised back east in New York City. He ran with a gang in the back alleys of New York and rolled bums and drunk sailors fresh off of ships from Europe.

One day, while rolling a gray-haired old sailor with rum in his gut and money in his pockets, he and two friends were caught by a New York constable named O'Reilly.

O'Reilly spoke to Johnny and said, "So it is a robber ya want ta be, lad. Well, you two are not worth a wit, but you, young lad. I been keepin' an eye on ya fer some time."

Without another word, O'Reilly turned the other two over to another constable and took Johnny into an alley nearby. There, he pulled off his thick leather belt and removed the holster. He pulled Johnny's pants and long underwear down around his ankles and beat his rear end until the young teenager was black and blue.

O'Reilly said, "Every time I catch ya in trouble, young lad. This'll be what'yer gettin'."

Johnny never got into trouble again and grew up wanting to be a constable. When he was fourteen, his family moved to Chicago, and he ended up there joining the Pinkerton Detective Agency and became one of their best agents in short order.

Ferrucio sat across from Deputy U.S. Marshal Chris Colt, and his deputy Man Killer, an unlikely duo in this situation. The two men offered to meet him for lunch, Colt's treat, at the place they really became fond of on an earlier trip to Denver, the very posh Windsor Hotel, which had been opened a few years earlier, in 1880. Built by a silver magnate, H.A.W. Tabor, the Windsor had a taproom with 3,000 silver dollars inlaid in the floor. The hotel also had 176 marble mantelpieces in it. The restaurant employed seventy well-dressed and well-trained waiters.

The menu featured items such as Sweetbreads Glazed, with French Peas and Tenderloin of Beef with Mushrooms; or Baked Filet of Trout, larded, Madeira Sauce, Parisian Potatoes; and English Plum Pudding with Rum Sauce, or Neapolitan Ice Cream.

Just to remember how things had been in Denver in the "good old days," the masthead on the menu read 1859 GRUB BEANS, BACON, HARDTACK DRIED APPLES, TAOS LIGHTNING.

Both lawmen did their job because they loved it and believed in law and order, but in actuality, both were very wealthy, especially Man Killer, whose wife inherited millions. They didn't care. It was the excitement and the import of their work that made them want to do it. Man Killer had an additional incentive. Chris Colt had been his mentor, close friend, and sort of older brother ever since he was a young teenager, and Man Killer was about as loyal and supportive a friend as you could ever find. The two men enjoyed the Windsor so much that they decided that they would pay top dollar to stay there whenever they were in Denver.

Colt looked up from his oyster dinner at the Pinkerton man and said, "So what's the story on this killing?"

The agent unwrapped an oilskin pouch and tossed a sheaf of papers and a couple of ferrotypes in front of Chris Colt.

Johnny said, "The victim's name is James Adams from Santa Fe. He had a small freight business where he only carried expensive, or priceless items for people with armed guards. He would also rig the delivery wagons to suit each particular freight situation. In other words, if your mama had a big hand-carved china closet full of expensive bone china, and you needed to move it from Santa Fe to Cheyenne, let's say, he was the man who would get it there unbroken and safe. You'd pay a pretty penny, though."

Johnny took a bite of prime rib and chewed it thoroughly, savoring the juices and taste of the good beef.

He went on, "The man was pretty solid, but he had lots of bills. High-debt ceiling. Anyway, he was plugged in the back by a big hombre that worked for him named Drago Meconi."

Colt said, "Fellow Italian, huh?"

"Not of mine, partner," Johnny interjected quickly, "This man worked for Adams and was supposed to be trusted. Paid well, too, better than most folk's wages. So how did he repay Adams? Put three .44s in the man's back and then a finishing shot between the eyes, point-blank. I don't want to claim him as Italian."

Man Killer said, "Did he have family?"

Johnny said, "That's the hell of it. Beautiful wife, name of Charlotte and two little girls. Married about five years, but we think she was in cahoots on the shooting."

Colt said, "Her, why?"

Ferrucio said, "Oldest reason in the world."

Man Killer added, "Money."

Johnny replied, "That's it. See, his best friend

growing up just happens to be the son of the Secretary of the Treasury. It seems they asked him several times to carry big army payrolls secretly in his wagons while carrying some valuable piece of furniture as a cover. When he got it in the back, they made off with a payroll of two million dollars."

"Why do you feel his wife is involved?" Colt asked.

"When we started checking," Johnny went on, "we found that James Adams never told anyone about carrying the army money. We figure his wife was the only one to know. Nobody knows now. It is to be kept totally quiet, period. When we started our investigation, we first got suspicious because we couldn't find out anything about her when we ran a background check. Then we found out this Drago Meconi met privately with Mrs. Adams twice in the week prior to her husband's death, while James was off to Denver himself."

Colt said, "Sounds awfully suspicious."

Johnny said, "Yes, it is. On top of that, Adams had paid off his home several years ago, but took out a loan against it and was behind in the loan when he was shot. On top of that, he also owed quite a bit of money at several expensive stores in Denver and Cheyenne and all for dresses and jewelry. We think she's laying low and will meet up with Meconi later on when things cool down."

CHAPTER 4

Man's World

Charlotte Adams opened the little hand-carved drawer of her jewelry chest. She reached inside and pulled out the very last piece of jewelry. She looked down at her two little girls, who were wearing her dresses and shoes and trying to walk around in the oversized clothing playing dress up. Charley smiled, then tears flooded into her eyes as she thought back to all the gifts her late husband showered her with. Charley was furious with him for spending so much money on her and their daughters, and she wondered how they could keep coming up with more money. Unfortunately, he handled all their finances and preferred not to let her know much about it, so she wouldn't worry when they were low on funds.

She would take the diamond brooch and try to

get some money for groceries and immediate bills. Edgar Northingham was the local banker who kept bothering her, and she was hoping he would not come by again this week demanding money.

Ever since James was murdered, Charlotte had been struggling to protect her little girls. Because of her own childhood and her stepfather, she was bound and determined to never let her daughters go through similar rough times.

After the funeral, the bills started almost immediately and so did the marriage proposals, two from wealthy men, but that was the last thing Charlotte Adams wanted. She loved her husband very much ever since she first met James in Cimarron when he was engaged to the uppity woman from back east. Charlotte couldn't even remember the woman's name right now. Five years had passed already. She was now in her early twenties and no longer the frightened young teenaged girl who had to be a woman so fast. She also had two daughters to be responsible for, and she was bound and determined to ensure they grew up properly.

Charlotte looked out the back door and saw Rebecca and Emily playing and giggling in the back, both had their sunbonnets pulled off and hanging on their backs. Charlotte smiled, then jumped as she heard a knock at the front door.

It was Edgar Northingham, the banker. Dressed in a gray pinstripe suit, with a diamond tie tack and gold watch fob, and prime beaver derby hat to top it off, he looked the epitome of wealth and power. Graying at the temples and developing a middle-age paunch, he was an inch shorter than Charley who ran a little tall for a woman, maybe five-ten in riding boots.

Charlotte wiped the dishwater off her hands and walked to the door, pushing a strand of golden hair back off her face, and straightening her apron. Giving her right hand one last wipe on the side of the apron, she reached out and opened the front door. Surrounded by rosebushes on either side of him, he looked quite the dandy standing in the doorway.

Charlotte said, "Mr. Northingham, what an unexpected surprise. Do come in."

He entered, and she offered him a chair in the living room, taking his derby and hanging it on a coat tree in the near corner.

"Mrs. Adams," he said, "I am your banker. I feel we should be friends. Please call me Edgar."

"Very well," she said, "only if you will please call me Charlotte. Tea or coffee, sir?"

"Coffee, please, two sugars," he replied.

She excused herself for less than a minute, returning with a small china tray, two cups, and a small pot of steaming coffee, as well as a sugar bowl and silver spoons.

Uncanny, Edgar thought, not only was this woman ravishing but just seemed to be as efficient as a queen bee. He wondered to himself how many women would have hot coffee ready to serve. When she set the tray down in front of him and poured his coffee, he could not help but stare at the large breasts concealed under the high bodice blouse. The only skin showing was part of her neck, but that was good enough for Edgar who had a very active imagination and extremely ugly wife.

Charley picked up a leather-bound humidor in the corner and silver cigar clipper and carried it to Northingham. She offered the humidor and opened the top.

Charlotte explained, "My husband always kept a good supply of cigars on hand for gentlemen who stopped by. James always said that there were few pleasures men enjoyed more than a good cigar."

Edgar immediately came back with, "Or a good woman."

His face turned bright red, and he almost spilled his coffee he was so embarrassed.

"Ex—a, excuse me, Charlotte, a—Mrs. Adams," he explained, stammering nervously. "I didn't mean for that to sound the way it did. I meant . . ."

Charley interrupted, "Mr. Northingham, relax, please? I know what you meant and took the remark properly. Is your coffee hot enough?"

"Indeed," he said, smiling, "it is very good indeed and hot as well."

She said, "Now, to what do I owe the honor of your visit, sir?"

Edgar clipped the end of his cigar and took a deep drag, blowing the smoke toward the ceiling.

"The smoke doesn't offend your nose, madam?"

"Nonsense," Charlotte replied, "I have always loved the smell of a good cigar. What I cannot abide by is the smell of whiskey on one's breath."

Edgar went on, "Well, Mrs. Adams, a—Charlotte. I have been going over your mortgage papers trying to figure out a way to help you with your situation. You know the president of the bank has already told me that I was to foreclose, but I know the deep loss you've suffered and want to help you out of this situation."

"Thank, you, sir," she said, "but how can you possibly help?"

He cleared his throat and poured another cup of coffee, taking a small sip.

"Well," he said, "please do not take what I am about to suggest in the wrong way, Charlotte. Well, the bank president has to answer to bank examiners, and he has, in fact, ordered me to evict you and seize the property."

Charlotte had been brave long enough. She simply broke down and began sobbing. Edgar slid closer and reached out rubbing her shoulder. He handed her a linen handkerchief with his other hand and she sobbed even more.

Between sobs, Charley said, "What am I going to do?"

Edgar said, "I don't believe it is entirely too late, Charlotte. I can help you."

Charley stopped crying and looked up, her curiosity piqued.

"How?" she asked.

He replied, "Well, it's quite simple. I am a man of considerable means, and you are on the verge of poverty right now, because of the debt load your husband left you. It cannot be a surprise to you, Charlotte, that you are regarded as a very handsome woman, very handsome indeed."

"Whatever are you talking about, Mr. Northingham?" she asked, now starting to get angered by the way the conversation quickly turned.

Edgar was in too deep now, though, and he was too full of lust and desire to even notice her mounting anger.

He went on, "Well, Charlotte, maybe you could just stay here and continue raising your lovely daughters in peace and tranquillity, and I could quietly help you with your bills."

She said, "And why would you want to pay my bills, Mr. Northingham?"

"Well," he said, clearing his throat again, "you and I could be just close friends, real close friends, and it would be a secret we could share. No one would have to know. Well, I believe it would benefit both of us."

Charlotte stood and said quietly, "I see. And your wife would know nothing about our friendship, huh?"

He got excited thinking of the possibility, replying, "Of course. We really wouldn't want to share that with her."

Charlotte extended her hand to shake and said, "Can I come to the bank tomorrow and give you my answer to your proposal? Let's say at ten in the morning?"

"Certainly," he replied, "think it over by all means. We'll talk tomorrow."

She walked to a rolltop desk, and got a pen, ink bottle, and notepad, returning to the banker, who was now standing.

Smiling seductively, Charlotte said, "Now, Edgar, would you jot down for me just how much you think you could afford to pay on my bills each month, if I would become your special, a secret friend?"

"Of course, my dear," he replied, "of course."

He quickly wrote what came into his head and handed the pad to her.

She said, "This looks fine, Edgar. I'll see you at your office tomorrow morning."

He walked to the door and turned, hand on the knob, "I do hope you will let me help you? I really want to, you know?"

She smiled sweetly saying, "I believe you really do. Good day."

She closed the door behind him, checked on her girls, and ran into the bedroom, throwing herself on the bed and crying her eyes out.

Mrs. Northingham was puzzled by the note delivered to her from Mrs. Charlotte Adams, as she had never met the woman, then she figured out who she was. She was the widow of the man who had been killed and held up with the valuables from the freight line, the handsome James Adams. Mrs. Northingham met him one time when he made a delivery for a friend of hers. He was a handsome man and a perfect gentleman, and she was quite impressed.

The note asked her to meet Mrs. Adams and her husband on Thursday morning at ten a.m. at her husband's office, and she was not to let on about it with Edgar. Maybe it was some sort of surprise for him, but his birthday was months away. In any event, she decided, she would be there.

The next morning, Edgar was very surprised when he greeted Charlotte with an enthusiastic welcome and suddenly his wife showed up. Charley carried a chocolate cake she had baked. She set it down on the edge of his desk and met Mrs. Northingham at the office door. Edgar was pleased at first by the cake, but then started seeing what was going on and began to squirm. Charlotte bade Mrs. Northingham to enter the office and be seated. She closed the door behind the woman and sat down herself opposite Edgar.

Nervously, he said, "Mrs. Adams, how nice. I see you brought a cake."

Charlotte stood and smiled sweetly, picking it up, and saying, "Yes, I made it especially for you, Edgar."

She turned her head to his wife and explained, "He insisted I call him that, because we are special friends. Aren't we, Edgar?"

Charley dumped the cake on top of his head and angrily said, "I made this for you, because I wanted you to know this is the only thing you'll ever get from me, even though you tried for a lot more."

The woman gasped and Charlotte turned to her, handing her the note he had written down.

Charlotte said, "He offered to pay my monthly bills and mortgage, if I could be his quote, special friend unquote. As you see on the note, that's his handwriting, and he wrote how much he would be willing to pay each month to be my quote special friend unquote."

Edgar couldn't speak and looked, red-faced, from his wife to Charlotte and back. Charley then noticed something she didn't expect. Edgar not only got red-faced, his veins started bulging. He got furious.

Mrs. Northingham, also angry, said, "What is the meaning of this, Edgar?"

Edgar totally shocked Charlotte by saying very firmly, "Be quiet, Margaret. Be quiet and go home."

She said, "You invited this woman to have an affair with you, and you dare tell me to be quiet!"

He stared daggers at his wife and gritted his teeth tightly, saying, "Go home to your big house, servants, gardens, the club, the balls, and dinner parties, unless you've grown tired of those things. Go home and never stick your nose into my business again."

The woman huffed, but the words struck home, and she quietly got up and left the room without looking at either of them.

She stopped at the door, as he spoke, "Have a nice hot dinner ready when I get home."

Totally humiliated, she barely spoke above a whisper, saying, "Yes, dear."

Charley could not believe it. This was one thing she hadn't counted on. She knew that other women were very subservient to their husbands, but she had never had that kind of relationship with James Adams.

They were more like partners, and her opinion

really did count with him. They shared everything, and the only time he didn't listen to something important that she had to say it cost him
his life. She told him about Drago Meconi coming to their home while James was away and trying to hint around that she have an affair with
him. The second time he came, he out and out
suggested it, and was quickly sent away by her
with some very sharp words. She warned James,
over and over, that he couldn't trust the man, but
all James would do was defend Drago. He spoke
of the several years of unflagging loyalty of
Drago and saw so much good in others, he just
couldn't believe that the man could not be
trusted.

It had hurt Charley deeply that James
wouldn't believe her, but this was different. Mrs.
Northingham did believe what she was confronted with, and she had tried to stand up this
time apparently. The problem, however, as
Charley saw it, was that the woman did not have
the wherewithal to stand up to Edgar and not
back down. She liked the money, prestige, and
comfort that went with being his wife. Charlotte
just could not believe that a woman could lack so
much gumption, but then again Charlotte had

been forced to have gumption, lots of it, ever since she was a small girl.

Edgar glared at her, an evil smile on his face.

He said, "Your husband put up all your furniture, everything you own as collateral on his last loan. That includes your home and land. I will give you one week to get the arrearages caught up or you and your daughters will be thrown out in the street, with just the clothes on your backs. You'll learn within the next week that you'll want to be my whore, Mrs. Adams."

Charley got up and walked up to him slowly. She swung as hard as she could swing her right fist from the hip and the punch caught him on the point of his chin. It felt to her like her knuckle on her middle finger was broken and her arm hurt all the way to the shoulder, the blow was so jarring, but she smiled as she saw the man topple backward over his desk and his feet caught on his leather chair, causing his face to slam into the floor even harder. Edgar started to get up but fell over sideways when he tried to stand. His eyes were glazed over as he held his jaw.

Charley smiled softly, triumphantly, as she walked over to the door and put her hand on the knob.

She said, "You're wrong, Edgar. I'll never be anybody's whore. You married the whore."

She walked out the door.

At her house, Charlotte Colt Adams gathered up her two daughters, and the clothes she could fit into a carpetbag. With tears running down her cheeks, she took her children to Mrs. McGovern's house, the sometimes baby-sitter in the past, and returned to her place alone.

Charlotte thought back to her time with the Apaches and fleeing from her home the night of her stepfather's death. She thought of the diseases her family had survived, and the many trials she and James had been through.

She looked skyward and vowed, "I'll make it through this, and my daughters will not have to put up with any wicked man that happens along with money. They will be well taken care of and will grow into fine young ladies. I will succeed. By all that's holy, I will succeed."

She rushed around the house, her teeth gritted together, and found every container that she could find with flammable liquid. She poured them everywhere she could around the house, on furniture, curtains, walls, floors, then without looking back, she walked out the back door and dropped a match into a trail of kerosene. The house already had smoke pouring out the windows before she even made it one block.

By the time Charley made it to Mrs. McGovern's house, she could hear the alarm going up for fire and shouts began in the distance. The kindly old lady patted her on the back, as Charley silently passed through the door and hugged her children. Mrs. McGovern led the three of them into the spare bedroom and quietly closed the door. Charlotte held her little girls and cried until she fell asleep, her arms around both girls.

Charlotte napped until early afternoon and she promptly returned to the house, which had now been burned to the ground. She walked on past the house and headed straight to the bank.

Entering the bank, she asked for Edgar and was told he was in a meeting with the president and other bank officers. She inquired about the board room and a tired teller pointed to a hand-carved oak door with large brass handle. Charley brushed past the teller and reached the door with protests and shouts being hurled, ineffectively, at her back.

Charlotte Adams entered the room and all noise stopped, as all eyes turned toward the ravishing blond woman with the tear-puffed eyes.

Charlotte walked around the table, her heels making loud echoes in the still quiet room. She walked up to a wide-eyed Edgar Northingham and dropped something in his hand. He looked at it and saw it was a house key.

Charlotte said, "Here's the key to your new house. Maybe you can invite you're friends here over for a barbecue."

She turned and Edgar, red-faced stood, shaking his fist, bristling. "Mrs. Adams, you're going to jail for burning down that house."

She turned and grinned, walking over to the bank president and said softly, "Maybe you should explain to your genius here what is going to happen in all the newspapers in the territory if a poor, newly widowed woman with two small girls is suddenly arrested after losing both her home and her husband, and she is arrested for burning down her home that the big old bank took from her."

Edgar shook and Charley laughed.

She walked to the door, and he started to say something, but the bank president cut him off, saying firmly, "Edgar sit down and be silenced, now."

Charlotte laughed loudly and walked out the door.

Charlotte picked up her girls an hour later, and they went by buggy to the outskirts of town to a large estate. The stone building and walled estate had a big sign set in stone which read WESTFORD SCHOOL FOR YOUNG LADIES.

After ten minutes in the waiting room, Charley and her daughters were led down an echoing hallway into a high-ceilinged, dark oak-paneled office with the walls lined with bookcases. All the classics were on the shelves, as well as numerous reference books. In the far corner was a very large desk, hand-carved in Germany and transported by ship across the Atlantic, and ironically, transported by James Adams by wagon from Denver after rails from the East. He also moved some of the more expensive pieces of furniture in the building, as well. At several functions, Charlotte had met Mrs. Westford, the very proper, but warm, gray-haired lady seated across from her now at the big desk.

The two spoke for well over an hour while Charley explained her situation and strong desire for her little girls to have a proper and secure upbringing. She was determined to take care of the tuition at Westford each month even if she had to sleep under bridges or trees for shelter.

Charlotte was so determined and sincere that

Mrs. Westford, gave her thirty days to come up with the first month's tuition fees. This was the woman who, years before, had learned to simply set tuitions, and it was the parents' responsibility to meet them. Every time she had extended credit or helped out individuals, she always ended up with an empty feed bag. The mind-set of Charlotte Colt Adams, however, was such that any person would be impressed, especially one who taught virtues like hard work and tenacity.

So it was that the young beautiful widow with the golden tresses left her daughters in the care of the elderly lady of refinement and gave them cheerful farewells. She didn't know that the man who had been watching her with the long spyglass, was watching her ride away from the girls' school in the buggy that brought her. Satisfied with himself, and his ability to follow and survey, utilizing available cover and concealment, the Pinkerton pushed his telescope back into its small tube and shoved it in his pocket.

Climbing down to his horse to continue his surveillance, he said to himself. "Well, you poor widow, enrolling your girls in the most expensive exclusive girls' school in the territory. It must be terrible for you financially."

When Charlotte returned to town from her

buggy ride, she took out her purse and counted out thirty-two dollars. That was what stood between her and starvation. If it was just her, she would have gone back to live with the Apaches. They treated her great, and she knew she would never starve with them anyway.

Charley, as in weeks past, walked up and down every street and read every handbill posted, looking for a job. At every turn, she was becoming more and more frustrated. If she was a man, she could find a job to make sufficient money to care for herself and her girls. The problem was that she was either propositioned, turned away, or told she was a woman and the available work was only suited for a man.

Charlotte thought to herself, if only she was a man, she might make it. That was a ridiculous thought, though, because if any woman did not even come close to looking like a man, it was Charlotte Adams. Her breasts alone would betray her long before anyone had a chance to look at her closely.

Charley was thinking about all this when she came around a corner and found a man tacking up a small handbill on the front of the marshal's office. She looked at the bill and tore it off, reading while she walked along. The job was for a young man to learn the freighting business, working between Denver, Fairplay, Colorado City, and Leadville, Colorado, for a mining conglomerate. The handbill said the individual had to be a "very fair hand at gunplay" as the work was quite dangerous, but the pay would be "just right for the right individual who wants to start young and grow with the company."

If only I was a man, she thought. Charlotte had an idea and headed to the dry goods and general store across the street for some quick shopping. Ten minutes later, she emerged and rented a room at a hotel down the street.

In front of the mirror in her room, Charley looked at her breasts and pressed them as flat as she could against her chest. For a few seconds she thought back to James pressed hard against her body and a tear ran down her cheek. She quickly wiped it away and attended to her task at hand. Charley took some light homespun cloth and started wrapping it around her chest. She used it to bind her breasts tightly against her chest. Satisfied, she pulled out the scissors she bought and started cutting the long golden locks, while tears ran down both cheeks.

Speaking to herself in the mirror, she said, "I

will succeed, and I'll do anything for my babies, even this."

A sob escaped her lips, as she watched the first long handful of blond hair fall to the floor.

She did consider keeping her hair long and pulling it up into a cowboy hat, but she knew that the wind could blow it off and might cost her a good-paying job.

An hour later, Charlotte reported to the Santa Fe House, where the interviews for the freighter job were being held. She wore baggy trousers and denim shirt, as well as a kerchief around her neck, cowboy boots, and a .44 Russian tucked into the waistline.

The man who interviewed her had a very thick European accent that she could not identify. He asked about her background in the freighter business, and she was thankful for listening to her husband so closely when he discussed his business. Charley was even more happy when the man accepted her challenge.

In the middle of the interview, Charlotte, who presented herself as Charley Anderson, and speaking with more faulty grammar than she normally did, said, "Sir, yer offering eighty bucks a month fer this job, which is a lot more than foreman's wages. There's plenty a pokes like me applyin'. Why don't we jest cut to the quick and let me go outside with ya and hitch up the team and freighter wagon ya had outside the hotel? After which, I'll give ya a shootin' demonstration, then I'll take ya fer a ride and show ya I can handle a team."

An hour later, after days of trying to find work, Charlotte Colt Adams, alias Charley Anderson, was the newest freight driver for the High Mountain Mining and Ore Corporation. She returned to the baby-sitter's, her only confidante, and changed into a dress and bonnet to hide her shortened hair. She immediately walked into town and rented a buggy, which she took out to the girls' school. There, she told the administrator of her happy news, promising money soon, and bade another tearful farewell to her daughters, explaining how much her work would keep her away. The Pinkerton agent following her was still trying to figure out who the small man was that had left the baby-sitter's house earlier and then returned. He wanted to figure out a connection between him and Charley and deduced that maybe the young man was a go-between for Charlotte and Drago Meconi. Thus far, the Pinkerton decided that she had planned for the two of them to lay low for a while, not spend any of the money, and wait for things to cool off. The agent, however, decided that he would not let things cool off.

Charlotte lay in bed that night, excited and scared. She had decided that she would land the job with the mining company for two reasons: the first was the money, but the other reason was so she could start tracking down Drago Meconi, the fiend who killed her husband. As far as she knew, Drago had almost always worked in the freighting business, or at least that was what was presented to James Adams when he hired the man. She figured if she started working in freighting, she may at some point run into Drago and when she did, she would shoot the man who backshot her husband.

The next morning, Charlotte and two other new employees, took the train north to Colorado City, where each of them was to meet up with wagons and senior teamsters, who would be the wagon boss. When they arrived they found that five other new teamsters had also been hired, two from Denver, and one from Colorado City.

All of them took off from Colorado City headed just north of Pike's Peak and over Wilkerson Pass, then on through Hartsel to Fairplay. There were still patches of snow on the ground at

Wilkerson Pass, but the trip was uneventful. In Fairplay, they dropped off supplies and some upgraded mining equipment for miners there, and loaded up with precious ore. After loading, they headed northeast to Denver by way of Kenosha Pass. In Denver, Charlotte went out for a beer after unloading with some of the teamsters. The place they went to was called Mulligan's and it was there that she got her first piece of information about Drago Meconi. She dropped several names, including his and someone in the saloon said that they knew a really big Italian-looking guy named Drago, but he was using the last name of Coppolla. They knew it was him, though, because he had briefly worked for a freight owner named James Adams and met Meconi there. Charley didn't know that Drago had stolen $2,000,000 from her husband. She also didn't know that he was laying low, like the Pinkertons suspected. He and his men had messed up the killing of James Adams, and he knew they were after him for murder, but he didn't know what was being done about the money, if anything. Drago was totally unscrupulous and could not see principle in anyone else. He became suspicious that James Adams may have stolen the money from the government somehow, and that was what Meconi counted on. If the freighter had indeed stolen the money, then maybe nobody would pursue him for that crime.

That much money had to bring many people after him, so he hid the money and would not spend any, at least for a while. Although, he did keep some money to use for his one passion and that was poker. He loved to play the game and lost often, like many who did love to play. He was good enough, however, to make him keep after the game trying to chase the money he had lost over the years. He had often used the excuse that he never had quite enough money, and he if he only had a little more, he would be able to play and win. That excuse was now gone, but he still chased what he lost the night before, almost nightly.

He was in luck because he had not been discovered, although he had taken a job on two different freight lines since the killing and was now looking for a job on the railroad, just to get away from what people associated him with.

Charley Colt carried with her a list of names of the three men with Drago Meconi and tried her best to recall what each looked like. Those three were in on the killing, she knew, because they were always with Drago and were thick like a den of thieves. She had warned James that they were up to no good, but James just simply thought better of people and never wanted to listen to her.

The list had the names of Piney Waters, who was a very tall, very thin, hatchet-faced man from the hills of Tennessee. He never bathed and smelled worse than a dead buffalo. The one time she met him, she smiled to herself when he spoke of Indians but referred to them as "stinking blanket niggers." Charlotte grinned, because she thought back to her time in captivity with the Apaches and remembered how clean they all were and how family-oriented. This contradicted so many of the myths perpetuated by whites around her for years. If she did not have her daughters to worry about and the burning passion now to get the men who killed her husband, she would have gone back to the Apache in a heartbeat. The life was hard, but it was also easy. The rules were simple and adhered to by a lot bigger segment of the society than it was with the so-called civilized white society.

The next man was Cyrus Minty. He was very short and very fast with a gun, always practicing. He looked to Charley like a picture she had seen of a baboon. His nose and jaw protruded and his eyes were very deep-set, and even his mannerisms reminded her of the monkeys she once saw in a circus. The man also liked to throw knives.

The third man was named Ezekiel Park, and he was a former slave from southern Georgia. Ezekiel was out and out mean and Charlotte assumed the man had had a very hard life and took it out on everyone else. She never trusted him, or the way he looked at her. Ezekiel was large and heavily muscled and had a very deep voice. He also had a bit of a stuttering problem.

It so happened that Chris Colt, Man Killer, and Johnny Ferrucio were now looking over the list of the names of the three men. They had been trying to locate them and had a little more information on them. Chris and Man Killer were going to venture down to Castle Rock, as they heard that Cyrus Minty had been hanging out there looking for a job with freighters passing to and from Denver. He probably figured that they would be more likely to look for him in the bigger cities or the major mining towns.

Castle Rock was between Denver and Colorado Springs and it brought back many memories to Chris Colt, and so did the man who he and Man Killer ran into on their way down from Denver. Colt didn't know where he knew the face from but there were mannerisms in the man's speech and the twinkle in his eye that made Chris realize they had met.

The man had hailed the two on the road and asked how far to Denver. He had been traveling up from Trinidad, where his son had passed from consumption. The man got a little sniffle when he mentioned that, but he had the look of a man hardened by many years in the hard west. He was so affable, the three rode into a grove of trees near the road and decided to eat lunch together. After the meal, Colt offered him a cigar and had one himself along with Man Killer.

The old man finally chuckled and said, "Chris Colt, ya don't member me, do ya? Ya shore have come a long way since you and me and the missus met. I read and hear 'bout ya all the time. Yer durned famous now. Member how Ma had kept me alive even though she was dead? Rest her soul."

Realization suddenly hit Chris Colt, and he and the old man, who still never gave his name, told the story to Man Killer over coffee. It had been after Chris Colt's first wife Chantapeta, Fire Heart, a Minniconjou Lakotah, had been killed by some renegade Crows. Chris Colt had tracked down the Crows one by one and dispatched them after they had raped and murdered the woman he loved along with their infant daughter Winona, which was Sioux for First Born.

Chris caught up with one of the Crows with a war party of other Crows who killed a man and his son and burned down their homestead. The man was in the process of raping the man's wife when Chris Colt appeared and beat him in front of the Crows war party and killed him with a knife.

Afterward, he had become romantically involved with the woman, Sarah Guthrie, and agreed to take her south to her parents' home in Cheyenne, Wyoming. It was 1876, shortly before Custer's death at the Battle of the Little Big Horn, or as the Lakotah, Cheyenne, and Arapaho allies called it the Battle of the Greasy Grass.

He met the old man out of necessity for transportation. He and Sarah had been riding double on Colt's horse before War Bonnet, a lineback buckskin named Nighthawk. Their journey took them southeast toward Cheyenne, but they had to avoid all the war parties and tribes moving to join up with Sitting Bull on the Little Big Horn for the annual sundance ceremony, something Chris still bore the scars from.

Chris recalled the journey vividly and wondered about Sarah. She was frightened and in shock at the time, having lost her husband and son so violently and quickly. She was scared going across the prairie and not by road that she was used to.

"Isn't there a well-traveled road not too far away that goes to Cheyenne?" she queried.

"Yes," he replied, "and we'll take it when we get close to the city, but any warriors looking for trouble will watch the road also. It will be safer going cross-country."

"Oh," she said and seemed to be totally satisfied with the answer.

They crossed the prairie, and it seemed to Sarah as though they would never get to Cheyenne. It seemed endless; it was the same all the way around in every direction, for miles. Near dark, they spotted what Chris had been looking for, a homestead ranch. It was the ranch of the old man now drinking coffee with Colt and Man Killer. Approaching the little structure, Chris spotted a draw that wound around the house and went on south beyond it. He took

Sarah and his horse into the draw and approached that way.

When they were parallel with the ranch buildings, Chris said, "You keep on south in this draw and stay in it. I'll catch up. If you hear any gunshots, you go until the draw turns and get out and head east. You'll hit the road to Cheyenne and you just turn to your right, that's south."

"If I hear any gunshots, I'll stay put and wait for you," she replied. "You'll handle it, but why can't we just see if these folks will let us spend the night here?"

Chris said, "Whoever is living out here all alone has to be pretty tough to survive all the war parties coming through that have seen the place. I don't want to take a chance on them getting ideas about you."

Fifteen minutes later, he walked up to the house and hollered, "Hello the house! I'm a friend and my hands are empty!"

In those days and in that place, that was the only sensible way to approach somebody's property without getting your head blown off.

Chris was surprised to see a slight old man with a toothless grin walk out the front door and signal Chris to come in. At the time, he had no idea he would again see the man this many years later. He thought any man living out there would not be around long but was soon to discover why the man was alive.

The oldster said, "Come on in and set yersef down, youngster. Come talk to Ma, she loves comp'ny."

Colt was totally puzzled as he followed the man inside. His heart just about stopped when he walked into the sod-roofed cabin and looked into the blank vacant eyes of the drying-out corpse of an old woman.

"Ma, we got a visitor," the old man said, then turned to Chris saying, "This is Sadie. She loves folks. What's yer name, young man?"

"Chris, a, pleased to meet you, ma'am," Chris replied, feeling sick in his heart, "Sir, I'm really in a rush. I have to get to Cheyenne in a hurry. I noticed that you and your lovely wife have several head of horses in the corral. Can I buy one?"

The old man didn't miss a beat, "Yep, the blood bay'll do. Ma, takin' this young man out to look at the blood bay! Gonna sell it to him mebbe, if'n he's got cash and knows horseflesh."

"I have a little cash," Chris replied, "but I do know horseflesh."

They got to the corral and the old man snaked out a loop on a rope hanging on a cedar corral post. He tossed it, and it landed deftly over the neck of the blood bay horse, which was really put together, as were the other horses.

The horse didn't move once the loop was around his neck. Chris and the old man looked at the gelding and Chris Colt was impressed.

"How much?" Chris asked.

"Yer Henry repeater, and I'll throw in a saddle and bridle fer the young lady ta use," the man said.

Chris was really taken aback.

"The young lady? My Henry repeater?" Chris asked.

The old man replied, "Yeah, the Henry repeater ya' got in the saddle boot on that nice lookin' line back dun the purty young lady's on."

The old man chuckled, "Don't need no money, Colt. Not every injun that comes 'round here is gonna leave a crazy old man be. Some of 'em might wanna shoot it out."

"How did you know about the woman and the horse, let alone the rifle?" Chris asked.

"Telescope," the oldster replied. "Did ya' really think ya' was gonna injun up on my place through the draw an' put the sneak on me?"

Chris laughed and replied, "Yeah, I guess I did."

Retelling the story, the old man laughed heartily about it again.

He said, "You must have thought I was mighty teched in the haid."

Chris thought back to the incident and the old man's words at the time.

The old man chuckled, "Probably figgered whoever could last out here has to be grizzly tough or plumb crazy, huh?"

Chris grinned and the man went on, "Guess, I'm a little a both, but this is my home, and I'm still here. My wife went under a month back, rest her soul, but she's helping keep me alive. Three war parties been through here in the last two weeks. Lot a Sioux and Cheyenne on the move. Won't mess with a loony bird, figger it's bad medicine. Heerd they're goin' to join old Sittin' Bull up on the Little Big Horn. Ya' got the look of a scout, probably awready heerd it, huh?"

"I've heard talk, that's all," Chris said.

"Take the damned horse," the old man said, "she can pay me when ya' git to Cheyenne. Her folks can anyhow. I'll go in fer supplies and such fore winter."

"How do you know about her?" Chris asked, really curious.

"I seen her from a distance, time or two," the old one replied. "Need to know who my neighbors are, even if'n they're twenty, thirty miles distant, 'specially since I used to see her in her folk's store all the time growin' up. She didn't lose her ol' man and that cute little 'un, did she?"

Chris looked down and kicked the ground with his toe, saying, "Yeah, but not Lakotah or Cheyenne. A band of Crows raising some hell. What kind of work do you do, Mister? Whatever it is, it takes brains."

"Oh, let's jest say that a lot of lawmen in several states liked to keep pitchers of me when I was younger and better lookin'. I'm retired now, but I'm fer sure they'd still like to find me and discuss them tintypes," the man said.

Chris caught up with Sarah an hour later, and gave her the smooth-riding horse. She was really amazed. He told her about the man and his crazy act while they rode south at a fast mile-eating trot. He got her back to her parents safely a short while later and had not seen Sarah since, but always wondered about her.

"You ever get down to Cheyenne and find out what happened with Sarah?" Colt asked.

The old man said, "Thet's funny. She ast me the very same question 'bout you jest one month past in Cheyenne. I seen her there and inquired bout her health. She has her a doctor husband and three young 'uns. Seems happy an healthy. We was both talkin 'bout how famous you got after we both seen ya last."

Colt said, "Well, I'm glad to hear she's doing fine. What brings you down here? Just the funeral? You sounded before like you were going to spend out your days in that cabin."

The old-timer said, "Wal, sir, I got ta thinkin' 'bout how I coulda had mah hair lifted, an plus the fact thet I had put Ma in such a sityation, I decided thet I would come down and turn mahself in in Colorado Territory where I was wanted, at least most recent, anyhows. I comes down and turns mahself in ta the constable in Denver, and he says nobody wants me no more. Too many years. How 'bout thet?"

Man Killer said, "When had you committed your last crime?"

The old man pondered and said, "Wal, I met ol' Colt here in seventy-six, and it must a been 'bout fifteen year for thet. Anyhow, I started drivin' freighters, which was what I done for years afore I joint the owl-hoot trail. Ya know I had a nice young gal and about the purtiest woman I ever seen in mah days joint me some years back, five, six years ago. Said she was yer sister."

Chris said, "My sister! I don't have a sister."

The old man, Cracker, said, "I think ya do, Colt. She said yer old man probably never tolt ya 'bout her."

Chris said, "What was her name?"

The oldster said, "Charlene, no, Charlotte Colt."

Chris asked, "What happened to her?"

Cracker said, "I left her one day down ta New Mexico in a small town. She needed ta learn how ta flap her wings an I warn't gonna be no help. I was jest tryin' ta git back into bein' civilized mah ownself."

He accepted another smoke and enjoyed a long draw.

Cracker said, "Ya know, thet youngster was so durned beautiful, I couldn't never speak ta her hardly. I ain't never seed a woman fore or since could take a man's breath away like thet."

Colt said, "You sure she wasn't joking?"

Cracker said, "Absolutely."

Colt said, "Absolutely sure she was or wasn't?"

Man Killer started laughing, saying, "Great

Colt, Joseph used to say if the mare kicks you, do not ask her to kick you again to make sure she wanted to kick you."

Chris laughed at himself, something great men seemed able to do.

Cracker chuckled and stuck a long weed in the corner of his mouth, chewing on it lightly.

He said, "Ya know, she does favor ya some, although yer one ugly ol' horse thief and I swear. I mean Ahma here ta tell ya. This little looker had long, curly blond hair that was the color a honey with the sun shinin' on it. Her eyes was as blue as the sky on a nice day, and she really did have that slant ta her eyes you got, plus thet smile in the eyes like you got."

Colt said, "What smile?"

Man Killer laughed at this question, replying, "You don't know? Your eyes always smile like you know a secret no one else knows."

Cracker said, "Ya know. Thet describes it sure enough, Man Killer. Wal, let me finish tellin' ya 'bout this young gal. 'Course, by now, she'd be in her early twenties. She had an upstairs on her thet looked like it was built fer a much bigger home, and dint need no first floor to hold it up neither, if ya know what Ah mean. Oncet, after we crossed the Llano Estacado, and she was washin' up in a stream, I happened ta come down ta wash out mah drawers and sech. Wal, she was dressed right skimpy in thet water, an she had legs what looked like she had been squeezin' a horse's sides bareback an awful lot. Now, I acted proper an got away from the stream, but not a fore I did notice some skin what was put on right proper."

Colt said, "Do you have any idea what happened to her?"

Cracker said, "I 'spect she got married an had her a passel a kids. What else would a purty gal do?"

Charley Adams, alias Charley Anderson, stared at the baboon-looking face of Cyrus Minty. She had seen him several times working for her husband, and she knew that he had been involved in the murder of James. All Charlotte could think about was pulling her pistol she had been practicing with over and over, every chance she got. As she thought about shooting the man, her hatred and anger welled up even more, but she also visualized shooting a man dead and Charley literally got sick to her stomach. The more her nerves played on her, the sicker she got and was soon leaning over the side of the freighter and vomited. This was done right on the main street of the little town of Castle Rock, and a woman about fifty years of age was walking by on her way to the dry goods store. When she saw Charley throwing up off the wagon seat, it made her sick, and she started vomiting as well.

Charlotte jumped down off the wagon seat, ignoring the senior freight driver, except to give him a wave of her hand over her shoulder, as she followed Cyrus down the dusty street. The driver just figured she was sick and was looking for an outhouse. He was planning a cold beer or two anyway, then getting a room before continuing on to Denver the next morning.

Cyrus, oblivious to his stalker, had his own plan. There was a nice little house down the street, actually a well-chinked log cabin with cloth partitions throughout serving as walls. In the large cabin's interior were a number of young ladies whose favors could be bought for very little money. That was what Cyrus had, too, because he did not know about the giant army payroll stolen from James Adams. He thought he had received his share of a ten-thousand-dollar express box that James was carrying. Cyrus was entirely happy with his share, but he was near the end of it. The man had been warned to wait to spend the money, but he was in a poker game the first night after the murder of James Adams. Since then, he had lost a couple thousand dollars, which was about all he had. Minty didn't care. It was the fun of acquiring the money that thrilled him. He was also, like most outlaws, very lazy and hated to work. He would use most of the money he had left to hire two women to celebrate with him in one of the little cubicles.

Charlotte had no idea what she was going to do except that she had just discovered one of the men who was involved in murdering her husband. She was going to do something. She had to.

Charley Anderson entered the large cabin/brothel. A buxom red-haired woman immediately approached her and acted flirtatious. It took Charley aback, until she realized that she did indeed look like a young man.

The woman, with a pockmarked face that would have been pretty otherwise, said, "Hiya, Sonny. Lookin' for some real lovin'?"

Charley said, "No, just looking around a second."

The woman stepped up to Charley and reached down grabbing her crotch. Charlotte almost screeched and grabbed the woman's wrist, roughly. The redhead screamed in pain.

The madam gritted her teeth and forced a smile, saying, "Hey, I felt what you got down there, Mister, and there's plenty of us girls here that would love to have you. Got your poke?"

Charlotte said, "Lady, keep your hands to yourself."

Charlotte turned and quickly walked out the door, propping herself against the side of the building trying to catch her breath. She walked over to a well about twenty paces from the front door and sat down, her back against the side of the well. Charley was in shadow.

There was a creaking sound and Charley's eyes popped open. She had been asleep. Now, she sat bolt upright and saw the figure of Cyrus Minty, not more than fifteen paces away. He closed the door behind him and looked up at the stars overhead, stretching his arms and yawning. He pulled something from his pocket and fiddled with it a few seconds, then a match flared, and she watched him light a cigarette. Cyrus took a long drag and blew the smoke skyward and did not see the figure of Charley standing in front of him.

She said, "You shouldn't stare at a match or a

campfire at night without closing one eye, Cyrus. It makes you night-blind."

Minty jumped a bit, then chuckled with a nervous little laugh.

He said, "You scared me a mite there, Mister. I didn't see you in the darkness."

Charlotte, without even thinking about her words, said, "That's fairer than the way you and your cutthroats murdered my husband. Draw!"

With that, Charley drew her own gun and started firing. Cyrus was so shocked, he failed to draw his own gun and finally did so, but he was still not seeing well in the darkness and the light from the muzzle flash blinded him even more.

Charley, frightened to death, just kept firing and shot three more times with the hammer clicking on empty cylinders without even realizing yet, that she had shot all six bullets and was out of ammunition. She ejected her empties and nervously fumbled to replace them with more rounds.

In the meantime, Cyrus fired in the direction of Charlotte but still couldn't see very well in the darkness. Charley felt something tug at her sleeve, and she dived to the ground, still reloading. Cyrus fired twice more and bullets kicked up dirt on both sides of her, but Charley steeled herself. She pulled the hammer back, lying on her stomach, propped up on her elbows. She carefully aimed at the center of the black shadowy figure in front of her and squeezed off a shot, then another, with each shot making the body jerk, and the last one slammed Cyrus against the door of the cabin, and he fell backward crashing with the door, light streaming out into the darkness. Charley stood briefly and saw the redhead stare at her, the woman's eyes open wide as saucers.

The prostitute held her hands up in front of her face and screamed, "Don't shoot me, please!"

Charlotte felt bile come up in her throat as she looked at the still body of the man she just killed, and she stumbled into the darkness. She vomited behind a small outbuilding, then ran as fast as she could out into the night, away from the lights and the town and the people. Charley ran and ran until she felt she couldn't breathe anymore. Outside of town, she finally dropped down on both knees, sides heaving. Charley lay there for a full five minutes and then suddenly the sobs started coming, at first they were short and hesitant. But soon enough, they came out in racking sobs. Charley pounded her right fist on the ground, while she lay her face across her left arm, still crying.

Behind her, back in the town of Castle Rock, she could hear the sounds of people yelling, talking, and horses' hooves pounding, as townspeople scattered to find the young, slight man who had shot down a visitor to the cabin brothel. The problem was that they were looking for someone on horseback, so common was that mode of transportation in the West. Escape routes were assumed, since Castle Rock lay a very short distance from the Rampart Mountain Range that started north of Pike's Peak and ran all the way up past Denver. The most highly traveled roads were south or north with essentially one main road coming in from the prairie out to the east. Assumptions were made that criminals headed north toward Denver, south toward Colorado Springs, then Pueblo, or into the mountains due west.

Charley's eyes opened wide, and she sat up. In the trees to her front was a small red light. It moved and her breath caught. She suddenly realized she had fallen asleep, actually cried herself to sleep. Now she was looking at the little glow of the end of a cigarette or small cigar in the trees to her front.

Survival instincts suddenly came into play, and Charley's right hand went down to her gun and holster that had been used so many times in practice for just such a day. The gun came up easily in her hand and was cocked. She aimed at the end of the cigarette and followed its slow movement up to a man's face. She could not tell in the moonlight, he was sitting on a log and looking in her direction. Charley could feel her heart beating hard in her temples and side of her neck. She could hear it pounding in her ears. She carefully aimed at the little orange glow. The man took a long drag on the cigarette, and it slightly illuminated his face. She was close enough to see that the man was ruggedly hand-some, and she could even sense wisdom in the man's eyes.

Chris Colt looked south and saw Pike's Peak in the distance with the bright moonlight reflecting off the bright snow covering its peak. He knew that they would head south the next day to Monument, and he thought back to Monument Pass and a very frightening journey across it. One that almost ended his life. It had occurred right after the Denver marriage of he and his beautiful wife Shirley, mother of his two kids, Joseph and Brenna.

A Colonel Rufus Birminham Potter, who was a very greedy and crooked land-robber had been outfoxed and outwitted by Chris Colt at every turn and was going to ambush the newlywed, with the help of his loyal foreman. The man had shot at Colt at long range, not knowing Chris had dressed mannequins in the clothes of himself and his wife and circled around the ambushers while they lay in wait. Both of the dry gulchers had made a quick trip to Hades, with the help of Chris Colt and his sidekick Man Killer.

Chris took another puff of his cigarette, and he suddenly tensed up. Something or someone was watching him, he sensed. He didn't know that his very own sister was just a few dozen paces to his front aiming a pistol at him right now. He got a weird feeling and shook in the shoulders as a cold chill ran up and down his spine.

Chris whispered to himself, "Come on, Colt. Relax for once."

He ignored the feeling, something he rarely did. This time seemed okay, though. Colt felt that, although something was watching him, he didn't feel as if he was in danger. He didn't feel stalked. That feeling of being stalked was a sixth sense that he and other warriors possessed, a knowing feeling that something was watching or stalking him. All people, at one time or another, have experienced it slightly, like when someone is looking through a window at them, and they turn around knowing someone is there. Real warriors, like Colt, learned to develop that sense to a keen edge.

Chris took another drag, and suddenly decided to cup the cigarette in his hand. Charley Colt watched the man in the trees take another long draw on his cigarette, then suddenly the little orange glow disappeared. Charley was scared and didn't know what to do, but she was sure that the man in the shadows couldn't see her. She, too, was in the darkness of a slight depression in the ground that ran right up into the trees. Charley didn't turn to see if the moonlight fell across her body anywhere, but she was reasonably certain that it didn't, and she darned sure wasn't going to make any movement. She simply waited.

Chris thought back to the first meeting between he and Man killer who now slept near their campfire back in the trees. A few lights blinked in the city of Castle Rock and occasionally, he could hear the tinny sound of a piano playing in a saloon. Above the town stood Castle

Rock itself, a lone rock-topped mesa amidst scattered foothills, their rounded tops covered with piñons, cedars, and pines.

Little did Colt know, three-quarters of a decade earlier, that the courageous young boy he was going to save would become his closest sidekick. Chris looked at the nearby Rampart Range and remembered riding the narrow canyon in Wyoming that led him to Man Killer.

He remembered riding through a really narrow part of a deep gorge. The rifle shot echoed off the black rock canyon walls and bounced upstream like a wildly ricocheting bullet. The battle was fierce, and Colt tried to identify the weapons by the sound of the gunfire. He was very careful as he walked his big black-and-white paint down the fast-running white-water stream. He had been following the tracks for several hours, simply because this was some of the wildest country in the American West, and he wanted to make sure that he knew who was near him in the neighborhood.

He had rendezvoused a few days earlier, with his blood-brother Crazy Horse in the Yellowstone and killed a giant of a man named Will Sawyer, who was very much in need of killing. He was now traveling west but had cut down through the Grand Tetons, deciding to take the easier route to Oregon along the Snake River going by Boise. His destination was Fort Lapwai, where he was to report to old "One-Arm" himself, Brigadier General Otis Owen Howard, who the soldiers all called "the Bible-reading general."

The stream he now rode down was teaming with brook trout, rainbows, and cutthroat and had provided him with some good eating for breakfast. Usually when he traveled, he seemed to be under some kind of handicap. He was wounded, starving, had people chasing him, or was suffering some kind of hardship, but this day, he felt pretty good. He did have to leave the woman he loved at that time, Shirley Ebert, at her restaurant in Bismarck, North Dakota Territory, but she vowed that she would always be there for him, and he would return. Of course, he did and had now been married to her for some time.

If he would have known how the day was going to turn out, maybe he would have stayed upstream and fished all day, Colt figured.

The sounds of gunfire kept getting louder and the echoes were now passing beyond him going up the vertical canyon walls. The mountains all around were very majestic, very straight up and down, and very unforgiving. They were the Grand Tetons in western Wyoming. These were not gentle, easy-sloping mountains, like the Rampart Range, or the Front Range foothills where Man Killer and Colt now camped, but were harsh black granite sentinels to the Far West. Snowcapped and treeless halfway up, they went straight up to the clouds, and the Creator didn't stop to worry about travelers' ease and comfort when he created them. He did, however, think about something to rest your eyes on and take your breath away when you've had a hard day of pushing cows, hunting buffalo, or riding on patrol.

The tall man knew that the gunfire was now coming from just around the bend in the canyon wall. Movement. Two bald eagles came up the canyon, apparently spooked by the incessant gunfire. They flew overhead, and Colt couldn't help but think about what a good totem that was for most Indian nations.

He pulled his Henry rifle out and jacked a round in the chamber, eased the hammer off, and held it across the swells of his saddle. His sixteen-hands-tall horse knew that something was up, and he seemed to pick his steps more carefully. Nostrils flaring, War Bonnet's ears were pricked forward to hone in on any sound, no matter how slight.

The man whispered to his horse, "What do you think, War Bonnet, will they notice us?"

He laughed at his own joke. War Bonnet had been a gift to him from Crazy Horse, and ever since, he kept the same accoutrements on the well-put-together mount. More specifically, besides being a paint with a lot of white on him, he also had three red coup stripes around each foreleg, a red handprint on each rump, and several eagle feathers attached to his mane and tail. Whoever was in the battle around the bend would more than likely notice him. Colt still rode the same horse and kept the same decorations on him as tribute to his old friend and to the Lakotah, his adopted people.

In those days, Christopher Columbus Colt was a sought-after chief of scouts for the U.S. Cavalry and could easily follow the trail of a shadow through a dark canyon on a moonless night.

Colt eased his course around the bend following the tracks of the numerous unshod horses he had been following, with five sets of shod horses following the unshod ones. He knew exactly how many people were there, their sexes, and their nationality, because he was an excellent tracker and scout.

In those earlier days, Colt's exploits were fast-becoming legendary. He could read a track and figure out an entire story from it.

By following the tracks for a number of miles, he had seen that five white men were pushing a herd of unshod horses. Not only that, he knew that the horses were spotted. The reason he knew that they were spotted was because the herd climbed over and around rocks without slips or falls, where other breeds of horses would have balked at even crossing that rough terrain. The horses were Appaloosas, the spotted breed of mountain horses developed by the Nez Perce nation of American Indians. He also was able to tell that two more unshod horses were following the herd and these two had riders, both young, both Nez Perce. The moccasin tracks were similar to those of the Lakotah (Sioux) or Chyela (Cheyenne), except that the braves in those two tribes walked more pigeon-toed, but the Nez Perce walked with their feet pointed straight ahead. Also, because of walking more in mountainous country the Nez Perce walked with the heel first and toe second, but the Sioux and

Cheyenne walked just the opposite when stalking an enemy.

These two young people were stalking the white men. The rider saw several places where one of them would leave the trail, ride to higher ground, hide his horse, and sneak to a vantage point to watch the white quarry they were following. The tracker assumed they were young because of the lightness of their bodies and small size of their tracks. He figured one was around twelve years old and the other around ten. He knew they were boys and not girls because of some of the stalking techniques they had employed that would have been taught to young boys by older warriors. Things such as following the herd without walking over the tracks, but instead walking to the side of the tracks. The reason for this was to keep from spoiling any possible clues hidden in the trail and to help avoid being discovered by someone checking their backtrail.

The gunfire stopped, and then Chris heard the sound of voices and laughter. A few minutes later, he rounded the corner and stopped his big paint. The gorge widened out into a small bowl, and the herd of colorful horses milled around.

Two young Indian boys were in the midst of

five very rough-looking characters. Three were bearded, one was baby-faced, one was Latin in appearance and had a black mustache with very long ends extending well down below his jawline. Two of the bearded men were black. All five wore dirty clothing and guns in holsters that had been well-used. The Mexican was short and wiry, while the other four looked like they had easily pulled stumps out of the ground many times.

One of the black hombres held the older youth and laughed with the others as the baby-faced man held the ten-year-old by the throat and punched him repeatedly in the stomach. The boy's body was limp and lifeless, blood pouring from his mouth, nose, and right ear. He grabbed the boy by the legs and held him high overhead ready to toss him against the rocks, when Chris Colt fired a bullet right into the man's chest, and he fell dead, the boy landing on top of his bloody body.

The other four stared at him as he rode slowly forward, his Henry trained on the group. They thought about going for their guns, but to a man, realized this was no dude. They raised their arms, and when they did, the twelve-year-old spun, yanking the knife out of the belt of the man who held him and rammed it to the hilt into the man's midsection. The black cowboy's eyes opened wide in horror, and he stood straight up on his toes, a long low howl coming from his mouth. His mouth suddenly twisted into fury and the man took two steps forward, his arms outstretched, ready to clutch the throat of the young lad in his beefy hands and squeeze the life out of it, while his own drained out of his body. The boy stood his ground and spit at the outlaw, but the dying man kept coming forward. Chris Colt trying to control his own fury, fired a shot at the feet of the outlaw, but he ignored it and grabbed the boy. Colt shot him through the head, and the rest made sure their hands were high in the air.

The Nez Perce lad kicked the dead bodies of both men, then checked the heartbeat of his little partner. He looked sad. His eyes met the big white tracker's, and he shook his head "no." Chris felt a fury inside that was hard to control. He could not believe that these men had just killed a ten-year-old boy, simply because of racial hatred. The boy walked over to the tracker and turning, stared at the remaining men with deep hatred in his gaze.

Until now, nobody had spoken, but finally one of the men, the white bearded one said, "Yer damned sure biting off one hell of a hunk a tough jerky here, Mister. What's yer name?"

"Colt, Christopher Columbus Colt, but my friends call me Chris. You can call me Mr. Colt. Drop your gun belts."

The men all got a surprised look on their faces when he said his name. This man was a legend already, and he was still relatively young.

He signed to the young man, "Go-get-weapons-bring-to me."

The Nez Perce boy, who was actually a little past twelve and was Man Killer, except named Ezekiel then, scurried to each man and picked up their variety of weapons, belts, and holsters. He brought them to Colt and dropped them at the feet of the big paint horse, War Bonnet.

Colt looked at the Mexican and said, "Okay, amigo, what's the story?"

The man said, "Colt, we just were hired to."

Colt said, "I told you gentlemen that you can call me Mr. Colt."

The Mexican sneered and said, "Like I say, Colt, we were."

Boom!

The Mexican fell on the ground screaming, blood running out around the sides of his hands and between his fingers, while he grasped what was left of his right ear. He stood up again, pulling his kerchief off with his left hand and pushing it against the bleeding ear.

Colt was a tough man. You had to be tough to accomplish what he had, and he knew men like this. He had dealt with these types before, so he knew that he had to get and maintain the upper hand. If he showed any sign or indication of any type of weakness at all, he and the Nez Perce boy were dead. These men were like buzzards, or more like a pack of coyotes.

Chris Colt, sitting under the tree smoking and listening to the night sounds, thought about Drago Meconi and the men with him. He knew that this group of men had to be as bad as the men Colt confronted, years back, in Wyoming, and he thought back to all the various gangs of men he had encountered over the years. It seemed as though he was always outnumbered, but Chris Colt was still very much alive, and many of those men he had faced in the past were in Boot Hill or unmarked graves all over the West. He wondered what would happen if, and when, he caught up with Meconi and his men.

CHAPTER 5

Horse Thieves

Chris returned to the fire and poured another cup of coffee and lit another cigarette with a firebrand from the campfire. While doing so, he tightly closed his left eye, so when he returned to the darkness, he would not be night-blind. By closing one eye, while facing the fire, then opening it in the darkness again, his other eye would make him refocus almost immediately to the darkness around him. He returned to his spot on the log and looked out over the sleepy town while drinking the coffee and smoking. Man Killer and Colt sometimes took turns keeping watch at night, but this really wasn't one of those nights. Chris was just restless on this particular night and wanted to spend some time just thinking. If anyone would sneak up on them, the horses would warn them.

They were better than watchdogs. The herd Colt helped recover when he saved Man Killer as a boy was from Chief Joseph's original herd, and the horse Man Killer rode, Hawk, was one of the best bred down from the original stallions in that herd.

Chris thought back to that time.

He had just worked as chief of scouts for the recently deceased General George Armstrong Custer of the Seventh Cavalry. Having become good friends with Crazy Horse, Colt had first gotten in trouble with Custer and was arrested because he wanted to save his new love, Shirley, who had been kidnapped. Chris escaped, then was captured and held by Crazy Horse and witnessed the death of Custer and his command at the Battle of the Greasy Grass, as the Indians called it, but better known to whites as the Battle of the Little Big Horn. Because Colt was sympathetic to the plight of the red man, he was cautioned by both Sitting Bull and Crazy Horse to never tell he witnessed Custer's fall or white people might question his loyalty. In actuality, he was prepared to fight against Crazy Horse or anyone else, alongside Custer, the man he hated and despised.

Because he had gone after Shirley and returned with her after she had been kidnapped and traded to the Sioux, he was an even bigger hero in the white community. When he and Crazy Horse met, Colt had had his horse shot out from under him by Crazy Horse's warriors and was very courageous in facing the many braves. His courage impressed Crazy Horse, the famous Ogalala war hero, so much that the warrior gave Colt his own prized horse, which the Seventh Cavalry's stablemaster named War Bonnet.

Colt had gained the respect of the Apache, the Utes, the Comanches, Lakotah, and Chyela (Cheyenne), as well as the whites. He had already become a legend and was still "many, many moons" under thirty. Now, this legendary scout was on his way to help, as Chief Joseph and a small group of the Nez Perce were threatening trouble for the U.S. Cavalry and the white man in the Northwest. Feared and respected by white and red man alike, the only man for the job of chief of scouts was Chris Colt.

The young boy knew that he had to help this big warrior help fight the enemies, so he would mourn over the death of his younger brother later when it was safer.

Colt said, "What is your name, boy?"

The boy said, "I am called in your language Ezekiel."

He then added, "In my language my name means Boy Who Bites the Badger."

Chris said, "You speak English good. Learn from missionaries?"

"Yes, Catholic," Ezekiel replied.

"Okay, Ezekiel," Chris went on. "How about grabbing their ropes off their saddles, and we'll fix these gents up."

The surviving men were not in a mood to argue, or even chance blinking their eyes. Colt had made believers of the men.

"What is your nation?" Colt asked, already knowing the answer.

Ezekiel replied, "I am Nez Perce with the band of Hin-Ma-Too-Yah-Lat-Kekht."

The white man said, "Who the hell is that?"

Chris laughed. He didn't speak the tongue of the Pierced Noses, but he knew that name.

He replied, "Thunder-Traveling-to-Loftier-Mountain-Heights."

The man said, "What the hay?"

Colt laughed and said, "White people know him as Chief Joseph."

Chris looked down at Ezekiel who had gathered the ropes by now and said, "I am on my way to where your band lives."

Ezekiel said, "You go to work for the bluecoat father who has one arm."

Colt grinned and said, "How do you know I'm going to work for General Howard?"

Ezekiel laughed, "You said your name is Colt. All know the name of the great scout Colt. Joseph said you are like the strawberry that has been covered with snow."

Colt, surprised that Joseph had heard of him, said, "Why did he say that?"

Ezekiel replied, "He said that because you are white on the outside but red on the inside."

Chris laughed and climbed down from his horse, which stood still, ground-reined. The Lakotah used to put a very long lead line on a horse that was a herd leader, usually a mare. Whenever they had to gather a herd quickly, they simply went out and caught that one and the others would follow. Chris Colt taught his horse how to ground rein shortly after he got him from Crazy Horse. He simply buried a log under the ground and had a piece of rope with a snap coming up from the ground. He would ride the horse up to that spot and get off, dropping the reins on the ground. While the horse really didn't understand what was going on, he hooked the buried line to the chin strap at the bottom of the horse's bridle. Every time the horse tried to move, he would tug at the line and was unable to budge. It didn't take War Bonnet long to develop a behavior, so he wouldn't have pressure from the headstall on his poll, the back of his head behind the ears. He would stand perfectly still until his master came to him and gathered up his reins and mounted.

Chris thought about War Bonnet as he heard one of the two horses nicker as they munched on prairie grass to the east of Castle Rock. Charley had made her first move, slowly inching on her elbows and knees to where she thought the man, or men's, horse, or horses, might be. She realized how far out from town she was and decided to try to borrow a horse to return to town before daylight. She knew her partner would begin hitching the team at daybreak.

Colt took another long drag and recalled what they did with the outlaws in Wyoming. Colt had tied each of the men backward in his saddle. Hands tied behind them, the men had their hands tied to their saddle horns. They also were bound around the arms with numerous wraps, and each man had his feet tied into the stirrups and the rope was run under the horse's chest.

The Mexican protested, "I weel bleed to death, señor! Please?"

Colt laughed and said, "No, I believe you're going to die of hemp fever. You quit bleeding several minutes ago."

The white man said, "Hemp fever! You're gonna lynch us?"

Colt said, "No, but I'm sure the law will."

The black one said, "For what: killin' injuns?"

Colt said, "No, I didn't even ask Ezekiel here, but I guarantee you stole this herd of Appaloosas from the Nez Perce. Now, if you want, I'll take you to Chief Joseph instead of the nearest law."

All three got scared then.

The white one said, "I'll take chances with the law, a—Mr. Colt."

"Fine," Chris said. "I'm sure they'll be happy with you characters doing what you can to start a war with the Nez Perce."

The black one said, "What if our horse bolts while we're tied like this, or our horse falls?"

Colt said, "Then you might die. Should have thought of that before riding the owl-hoot trail, Mister. Honest men might not make big cash sums, but they usually don't have to worry about being tied backward on their horse, either."

Ezekiel said, "My brother Little Red Crow and I guard the herd. These men take. We follow. I must take ponies back."

Chris gave the youngster an appraising glance. He said, "You followed these crooks all these hundreds of miles. Did the camp know you followed them?"

"Yes," Ezekiel said, "I told them that it was my job to do. My brother followed."

"There is water, shelter, firewood, and graze. We will make camp in this place," Chris said. "Then we will make your brother ready for his Spirit Journey."

Ezekiel choked back his emotions and said, "It is a good thing."

Colt untied the three men and let them bury their partners. He also let the black one bandage the ear of the Mexican. Chris then went through their saddlebags, taking what ammunition he needed, and took their food out to use. The three men were tied to trees and a campfire was built. Colt wrapped the men in sitting positions with their blankets.

The white one said, "Mr. Colt, are we ta sleep this way?"

Colt said, "Yep."

The black one asked, "Are we gonna git fed?"

Colt said, "Nope."

The Mexican started to say something, but when Chris turned his head to listen, the man shut up quickly, thinking about his aching partially amputated ear.

Colt fixed a breakfast of beans, coffee, bacon, and biscuits. Afterward, he allowed the boy and himself a cigarette. He didn't smoke much, preferring cigars when he did, but occasionally the scout would roll a cigarette and enjoy it. With the Indians, tobacco was a real luxury and used in conjunction with spiritual ceremonies, along with relaxation.

The next day, they departed right after daybreak, leaving behind them a small valley containing the bodies of two greedy men and one small boy. The slate-gray cliffs shot straight up toward the heavens and acted as sentinels standing guard over the burial sites.

Chris reflected on that as they left the gorge. He thought about the many piles of bones he had seen, over the years, in the desert, out on the prairie, and up in the mountains. So many men, like himself, had left home at a young age and wandered toward the horizon where they had been watching the sunset every night. Colt wondered how many of those lost souls had wandered into a Comanche hunting party that didn't care for white-skinned intruders, how many had been struck by lightning out on the wide flat prairie, or how many had tumbled off a cliff into some lonesome gulch. The scout pictured families sitting at home, for years, wondering about the fate of a sister or brother with a wanderlust who hadn't answered any letters for several years. He wondered if he might become one of those unnamed skeletons some day. Chris Colt wondered how many people would miss him if he disappeared.

They pushed farther down the canyon, their minds set on the far-off Snake River. Colt studied the young Nez Perce lad out of the corner of his eye. The boy sat his Appaloosa proudly, eyes straight ahead, and back very erect. His young copper body blended into the rhythm of the spotted horse's movements, and Ezekiel, in effect, was "one with the pony."

The boy noticed Chris looking his way and gave the big scout a quizzical look.

Colt chuckled. "Quite an equestrian, aren't you, young man?"

"Huh?" the little warrior said.

Colt said, "Never mind."

They came down out of the rough rocks around noon and passed into a large valley choked with hardwoods and evergreens. Several ice-cold streams cascaded down canyon walls and cut swaths through the forested gorge.

Chris Colt loved the smell and sound as they rode through the stately pines and firs. He heard Ezekiel chuckling now and turned his head toward him.

The young warrior said, "I see it on your face, Colt. You are like the Nez Perce. You hear brother wind singing a song in the big trees and like his words. There, hear it? That way, the wapiti calls far off. He wants to fight another, for he is truly a powerful warrior. Up there, listen to it, Great Scout, do you hear it?"

Colt said, "A red-tailed hawk."

"He cries out to the rabbits down here," Ezekiel said. "Watch out! I am up here, and I am looking for you."

Chris said, "How do you know that he is not saying, 'Please don't attack me, rabbits. I want to land down there, but I am afraid of you.'"

Ezekiel laughed loudly and said, "He would never say that. For he is the hunter, and they are the prey. That would be like the great *Wamble*

Uncha telling these bad white-eyes that he is afraid of them and wants them to leave him alone."

The three men looked over at the boy, then the man. All three of them shook their heads, as if they had planned it like a synchronized cavalry troop movement.

East of Castle Rock, Chris Colt carefully extinguished the cigarette. He chuckled when he thought about the rhythmic, poetic manner of speech that Man Killer inherited from the great orator and leader Joseph. Chris and Shirley had, in fact, named their first child after the famous chief. Chris took a sip of coffee and savored the taste, remembering the conversation he first had with Ezekiel. He remembered that time in Wyoming, when he was attacked by a grizzly and was out cold for a long time. He had sent Man Killer ahead with the three outlaws and the herd of Appaloosas, then had to travel hard and fast to catch up with them, especially since the grizzly attack had left Chris with a concussion.

Colt had taken care of his horse, then prepared a meal. Chris finished eating, extinguished his fire, mounted his horse, and headed in the direction of the Pacific Ocean without a look back at the behemoth that almost took his life. He would canter and trot, alternating between the two paces and take a short break during the night. Colt would do this until he reached the boy and the brave young warrior's tremendous load of responsibility.

Colt headed down the canyon and hoped that the herd would move slowly and keep the Indian occupied chasing them into the gather. The going was very rough as the valley narrowed into another rocky gorge after just ten miles. Chris found where the herd of horses had to pick their way carefully through the rocks. He again respected Ezekiel for protecting the herd to save it for his tribe.

He kept pushing both himself and his horse but Chris was careful to watch warning signs with War Bonnet. He thought back to the horse he killed on his way home from the Civil War. He vowed then to always treat his horse as if it were the King of England himself from then on. The horse had pushed to a lather and beyond for many miles, too many miles when the young veteran came to the Tuscarawas River in southeastern Ohio. He and the horse started to swim the river when the exhausted animal's intestines twisted, and he died before making it across, going under and being swept downstream.

Chris Colt, the young Union scout and soldier sat down on the northern bank and wept, feeling more shame than anytime ever in his life.

Within the previous year, Chris Colt had already lost two other horses. First, he lost his dependable line back buckskin of many years named Nighthawk, when two men named Buck and Luke Sawyer ambushed him outside Cheyenne, Wyoming Territory.

A short while later, he had a sorrel cavalry mount shot out from under him by an Oglala Lakotah (Sioux) war party headed by none other than Crazy Horse himself. Colt's courage and spirit was so impressive to Crazy Horse that the famous Indian war hero gave Chris his own horse. When Colt arrived at Fort Abraham Lincoln, near Bismarck, North Dakota Territory, the Seventh Cavalry stablemaster gave him the name War Bonnet and suggested that Chris always leave the three red coups strips around each front thigh, red handprints on each rump, and leave the eagle feathers braided in the mane and tail, just like he was when Crazy Horse gave the horse to him.

Remembering that outside Castle Rock, Chris smiled softly as he heard a slight whinny from War Bonnet, who apparently had grazed a little too far away from his pasture-buddy Hawk. He didn't know that the big paint was actually nickering at the slight sound of Charley Colt Adams, alias Anderson getting a little bit closer. He and the big horse had been through a lot so far. Colt thought back to his search again for his new little friend in the mountains of western Wyoming.

That horse was drenched with sweat as it labored across the countryside, but he would kill himself if his master drove him to it. There was no danger of that, though. Colt had been checking the trail carefully and figured he was about four hours behind them, when he stopped for the night. He would only sleep for three or four hours, really just concerned about finding a place where War Bonnet would have good graze and water and a chance to rest for a bit. Hours before, the scout had found the place where the group had spent the night, so he knew it wouldn't be too hard to overtake them the following day.

Checking where they moved from their campsite, Chris was impressed with Ezekiel once more. Instead of worrying about pushing the herd and keeping them gathered, he had roped the lead mare of the Appaloosa herd. Ezekiel led the horse and the herd followed. Horses were very much herd animals and these spotted steeds were no exception. In fact, they had all been together since the birth of each, because of the culling and selective breeding of the Nez Perce who developed this special tough breed of mountain horse. The entire herd had followed Ezekiel and the lead mare. Colt also knew Ezekiel would have to move very slowly, because he was also leading three men tied to their horses.

He gave the horse as much rest as possible while he got several hours' sleep. Before daybreak, the scout broke camp after a quick breakfast and coffee. He started his fast pace again and traveled like that for two hours before stopping again.

Chris found another spot where the group stopped, and he halted to inspect the sign. Colt got very concerned now as he saw where the lad had apparently, for convenience sake, untied the black rustler and let him lead the other two.

The three men were just too worldly, evil, and clever for the young boy to let any of them have any freedom whatsoever. Chris felt real panic now, but he also knew he must pursue, yet be sensible about how hard he pushed his horse. Colt felt thankful that Crazy Horse had preferred large horses instead of the little wiry mustang ponies preferred by most Indians. War Bonnet was every bit of sixteen hands in height and his long-legged stride ate up the miles, as they continued after the young brave man and his vicious prisoners.

It was close to noon when Colt finally caught sight of the group. He topped out on a big rise and saw the men and herd in a grove of aspens down below him. The gorge had again opened out into a small mountain valley and Chris could clearly see numerous beaver dams and ponds below him in the wooded bowl.

The three men were loose and had a fire built. Ezekiel was tied to a small aspen, and they appeared to be burning him with flaming sticks from the fire. Chris could hear them laughing, but he could not hear the boy yell out in pain, at all. Even at that distance he could see the bright red blood on the boy's chest and on the light-colored dirt around him.

To this day, Man Killer still bore the scars from the ordeal.

It was combat again. Colt felt nothing but fury. Three grown vicious killers were torturing a small Indian boy. For what reason? He could not figure it out. He didn't want to. Colt wanted to just make them believers. He wanted them to know clearly that this young Nez Perce boy was a friend of his, and you do not hurt a friend of Christopher Columbus Colt. That is, you don't do that unless you are totally prepared to go to war; full-scale war.

Colt swung the paint off the trail to his right and into the aspens that ran up over the ridge-line and went on for a full mile. As he headed downhill paralleling the trail, he pulled his Cheyenne bow and quiver of arrows from his bedroll. He stopped and quickly dismounted, strung the bow, then swung back up into the saddle. When Chris reached the bottom of the hill, he angled to his left and dodged in and out between trees until he saw the smoke from the cooking fire.

Colt dismounted and weaved through the trees running forward. He got behind a large aspen and fired an arrow, watching until he saw it find its mark. The arrow took the black bandit through both upper arms and his upper torso, with just the last half of it still remaining in his body. He screamed so loudly and horribly, it made Colt think of the cry of a dying catamount. Eyes bulging and looking down at his paralyzed upper body, he stood up on his tiptoes, twisted, and fell face-forward in the fire. His body convulsed in further pain, then suddenly stopped moving. The others stared in abject horror.

When Colt was ambushed and lost his buckskin horse, Nighthawk, he found the bow and arrows cached near a spring and kept them. Prior to that, he had learned to shoot a bow expertly while living with the Lakotah.

The white man screamed, eyes wide open and the others dived for cover. The white one tripped, falling across the black one's body, burning his right forearm in the flames.

Colt laughed as he heard screams from them of, "Injuns! Injuns! Take cover!"

Colt ran downhill, quickly darting from tree to tree and dived headlong onto his belly, immediately scrambling forward on hands and knees. Chris made his way to an area opposite from the fire and looked more closely at the brave young Indian lad. He had a bloody knife wound in his chest and burns on several places of his body, but he looked like a young man playing tag and taunting someone to touch him. His lips were closed together tightly and his chin stuck out defiantly.

Man Killer had not lost any of his earlier courage or hardheadedness, either.

Chris moved expertly along on his elbows,

hands, and knees toward the end of a depression where he saw the Mexican disappear. He crawled into the furrow in the earth and faced toward the upper part of it near the campfire. Within seconds, the Latin rustler crawled around the bend of the draw and came face to face with Christopher Columbus Colt. He never said a word. His hand just streaked down for his gun and Colt released the arrow, which crashed into and through the man's forehead. He did not move. The arrow went through his skull and his head fell forward on the ground, and he simply lay there unmoving, very dead.

Chris got to one knee and looked around at ground level. Nothing moved. Nothing stirred. He heard a sound off to his left and immediately recognized it as a fox squirrel. His eyes kept straying to a large clump of brush to his right front. His mind automatically cataloged the area he saw the white man disappear into and this clump of thick brush was the closest and thickest cover.

Chris raised up on one knee and fired an arrow into the middle of the clump and listened. While up, he spotted the horses of the men and that was what would help him. He looked at the three horses the bad men had ridden and saw the horses all staring at the second clump of brush a little beyond the first. Their ears were all directed forward toward the brush, as well. Without hesitation Colt stood and drew his Colt Navy .36. He fired into the middle of the brush and the man stood holding a large red splotch of blood on his lower right side. He raised his gun with his left hand and tried to aim at Colt, but Chris's gun blossomed flame again and again and two more spots of red appeared in the middle of the man's chest. The .36 didn't have the knockdown power of Colt's mangled .44, but it definitely could kill. It did. His legs folded like an accordion, and he slouched to the ground, barely alive.

Chris ran to the boy, reloading his pistol on the run. His scalpel-sharp knife was out in a flash and cut through the young Nez Perce warrior's bonds like they were butter. All the while Colt never said a word but kept his eyes on the fallen white man. He moved to him, the Indian following.

The man was in obvious pain and shock and was trying to scream but couldn't.

He looked up at Chris and weakly said, "Shoot me, please?"

Colt grinned and said, "It appears that I already have."

The man looked at Colt with deep hatred and his eyes slowly closed. A wet spot appeared at his crotch. His entire body convulsed once and suddenly went limp.

Ezekiel looked up at Colt and smiled. His left eye was puffed up and blood was finally clotting from the wound. Chris led him back to the fire and had him sit down. The scout grabbed the dead bandit, still burning in the fire, and dragged his body off away from the fire and downwind from the duo. He had to block his mind out from the stench of the man's burning flesh. It was a hideous smell and Colt hated it, but this was certainly not the first time he had smelled it.

Chris added some small logs to the fire and broke out his coffeepot. He also retrieved the bone-handled knife the boy wore. It had been removed and stuck in a nearby log. Colt wiped the blade carefully on his pants and stuck the end of the blade in the fire. Ezekiel's eyes opened wide looking at his knife, but he checked himself.

He said, "Great Scout, why do you put my blade in the fire?"

Chris grinned and said, "'Cause I don't want to chance ruining the temper of my own blade."

As was the custom with most tribes, Ezekiel

didn't thank Chris for saving his life, but it was understood between the two.

Chris poured out two cups of coffee, after a few minutes, and gave Ezekiel one with lots of sugar poured in. He checked the end of Ezekiel's knife and saw that it was red hot.

Chris said, "I have to cauterize that knife wound in your chest, boy. That means . . ."

Ezekiel interrupted, "I do not understand big word, but I know what must be done."

"Want me to make you sleep?" Colt asked.

The boy said, "No, I am Nez Perce. Do what must be done."

Without further comment Chris moved the blade up to the stab wound and burned all the sides and edges of flesh and muscle that were exposed. Ezekiel stared straight ahead and didn't wince or make any change in his expression, but he was drenched with sweat in less than a minute. When Chris set the knife down, Ezekiel nonchalantly picked up his cup and took a swallow of the steaming hot coffee.

"Coffee good," he said.

Chris smiled and said, "You know how I make coffee?"

Ezekiel shook his head no.

The scout said, "I make it as strong as I can

and then add more powerful medicine to make it stronger. I know it is strong enough when I drop a bullet on it, and the bullet bounces off."

Chris held a bullet from his belt while he explained and shared a laugh with the Indian boy afterward.

The memory made Chris Colt grin and he decided to go pour himself another half a cup of his strong coffee, so he moved over to the dying campfire and chuckled when he heard a snore come out of Man Killer. The young man was, indeed, an Indian but he had just disproved the theory that Indians never made any noise at night. Man Killer's wife, the former Jennifer Banta of Westcliffe, could have told anybody that he oftentimes snored. It just proved what Chris already knew and that was that people are the same basically everywhere.

He bent over the fire and poured his coffee, but dropped the cup and whirled, guns in hand, when he heard a loud stick snap back in the trees, just past where he had been.

He stepped away from the firelight and whispered, "Man Killer!"

The deputy did not move a muscle and Colt could not make out his face in the shadow.

Man Killer, however, whispered, "What is wrong?"

Colt whispered, "Loud stick cracked north toward the horses."

Man Killer said, "Let's go," slipping out of the blanket and crawling forward rapidly and quietly.

Soon, he and Chris were covering each other, making their way by leapfrogging from tree to shadow, shadow to rock.

Standing by the meadow and spotting Hawk grazing peacefully nearby, Chris Colt said, "Damn!"

Man Killer said, "What is it, Colt?"

Colt was kneeling at the edge of the meadow, and cupped a match in his hand. Man Killer looked over his shoulder. It was clear that a light man had climbed up onto the back of War Bonnet and rode the horse away.

Colt said, "Small man, light, maybe just over one hundred pounds."

Man Killer said, "Maybe it's a woman."

Chris replied, "Maybe, but he's wearing working boots like freighters and miners wear. See the walking heels, too? We might as well get some sleep. Track War Bonnet tomorrow."

Man Killer said, "Do not worry. We will find him."

Colt said, "I know that, but my pride sure is hurt."

Man Killer queried, "Why?"

Colt said, "Look at our reputation, and somebody waltzed in here while I was awake and stole my horse. Damn Sam!"

"He was very, very good," Man Killer replied, then chuckled, "maybe his name is Colt."

The crash came shortly before dawn. In fact, it was the darkest time of the night, before false dawn. It was so sudden and so loud that Chris and Man Killer were both on their feet in an instant, pistols in their hands.

Another crash came as a giant lightning bolt hit a tree in the large clump of trees just across the meadow, rain and hail started pelting the pair, and they both quickly grabbed for their rain slickers. They put them on and huddled under some shorter thick trees. Both men did not have to be told to stay away from tall trees in a lightning storm. The downpour lasted for twenty minutes and gave the earth a very good and thorough, albeit harsh, scrubbing. All that the two deputy marshals could do was sit it out and be depressed.

Reading Colt's mind, Man Killer said, "Do not

worry. We lost the tracks, but we will find the trail. War Bonnet is not lost, Great Scout."

The latter expression was an old habit from their scouting days. He often referred to Chris, his hero and mentor, as "Great Scout."

An hour later, Man Killer mounted up and followed as Chris Colt desperately searched the ground for some small sign, anything to indicate which way his horse was led away, but there was simply no sign whatsoever. If there had been a piece of thread or cloth the heavy rains had washed it away after the large hailstones pelted it into the ground. There was simply no way for Colt to determine which way the horse would have headed.

Colt looked up at Man Killer, a hopeless look on his face. He knew the Nez Perce was thinking the same thoughts. Trackers could not only read different types of tracks and their ages, but they put all the information together to formulate an entire story.

Chris said, "You know what I'm thinking?"

Man Killer grimly replied, "Yes, the town of Castle Rock is too close. Whoever stole your horse may have been running from there or the law, but they would not ride a horse that looks like that into the town. It would be too easy to get caught."

Colt said, "The chance of finding him in Castle Rock is almost zero, but we have to try."

Man Killer didn't speak. He just stuck out his right arm and Colt reached up grabbing the man's forearm while his own was grabbed and he swung up onto the big Appaloosa behind his younger charge. They rode down to the near distant town and headed straight for the livery stable. There, Man Killer would grain, hay, and rub down his own horse, and they would inquire about anyone trying to sell a big, very noticeable paint.

The stable was at the south end of town toward Pike's Peak and the two men dismounted just outside the large weather-beaten double doors. There was a giant manure pile out back and a sluice trough carrying water from a nearby hillock, probably containing a spring. Water ran steadily into the troughs that provided water to three different corrals at once. The wooden trough extended into the stable itself, and Colt assumed that it continued on to provide water for other troughs that extended through each stall.

As the two men walked Hawk into the stable

Colt saw that his assumption was true, but more importantly, he saw a large black-and-white paint with two eagle feathers in his mane, one in his tail, red coup stripes around his forelegs, and red handprints on his rumps. Colt felt a lump in his throat. An old man walked out of a little makeshift office near the front of the building. He smoked a corncob pipe and had yellow tobacco stains in his white mustache.

Chris Colt had a killing look in his eye when he said, "Mister, that's my horse, and he was just stolen a few hours ago a few miles outside of town."

The old man said, "Then you'll be Marshal Chris Colt."

Colt said, "How did you know?"

The old man laughed at the silliness of the question. If Chris Colt and his horse were nothing else, they were noticeable, very noticeable and very famous. Chris realized this by the way the man laughed, and Colt chuckled at himself a little bit.

The man said, "Marshal Colt, I don't think the culprit that stole yer horse was all thet bad, maybe desperate fer a ride. He put yer horse in here and poured him a bucket of oats and forked some hay down ta him, whilst I was sleepin'. Then he left eight bits and this note."

The man handed the note to Chris, and he shared it with Man Killer. It read:

> *Dear Sir:*
> *Please forgive me for borrowing your horse, but it was an absolute emergency. He is a fine steed, with straight cannons, and handles like a Concord. I have left some coin for the stablemaster's fees, and even added a gratuity for the gentleman. I sincerely hope I did not cause you too much inconvenience.*
> *Again, my apologies, kind sir.*

Chris Colt smiled, saying, "Well, Man Killer, now we have a trail to follow."

Man Killer said, "And we follow a woman."

Chris said, "The wording of the note?"

Man Killer said, "And the handwriting."

The old stableman scratched his head and walked away, saying over his shoulder. "Well, yer bill's paid. Take 'im if ya want."

Chris said, "And she came from money."

Colt said, "How about the part here where it says 'handles like a Concord?' Tell me how does a woman know about driving a Concord?"

Man Killer said, "Maybe the note was written by a man, but the way she . . . Oh, I said she. It is written by someone who writes like a woman."

Chris said, "Remember that the man, or woman, was wearing boots you'd normally see on a freight wagon or mining? This note mentioned riding a Concord. I say that person drives wagons for a living."

The Concord that Charley referred to in the note was called by Mark Twain a "cradle on wheels." It was the very top of the line in stagecoaches. Even though it was in the 1880s, a Concord coach sold for $1,200 to $1,500, a lot of money in those days.

The Concord could seat nine passengers inside and as much as twelve people on the roof. Luggage was carried on the roof and in the boot in the rear. Valuables were carried in the express box in the driver's front boot. Inside, there were leather curtains and the very sturdy vehicle rode on two three-inch-thick leather strips called thoroughbraces. When the driver would stop the coach, he would rein the team of either four or six horses while pushing with his foot on the wooden brake lever on the right side of the boot. This would cause the brake shoe to push against the steel rim of the right rear wheel. The Concord stood just over eight feet in height and weighed better than 2,000 pounds.

The two lawmen both looked over the note some more, and Chris suddenly folded it up.

Colt said, "Well, you know a hard trail is like tough jerky. Let's chew on it awhile and talk about it later."

Man Killer said, "Saloon or marshal's office?"

Colt said, "You always learn more in a saloon than anywhere else."

They stuck their heads in the door and tossed the stableman some more money, telling him they would leave the horses there for a while. Colt set his saddle, which he had carried, on the top stall rail and petted War Bonnet, while Man Killer unsaddled and rubbed down Hawk. They gave Hawk some grain and forked hay down from the loft.

Afterward, the two headed toward a saloon that offered cold beer and food. They were both hungry and ordered beef steak, eggs, biscuits, and coffee. The two men sat there eating seriously and listening to conversation around them. Everyone was talking about the shooting, and they finally heard the name, Cyrus.

Man Killer said between bites, "We go to the marshal's now, huh?"

Chris winked.

After they got the story of the shooting, they went to the brothel to interview the madam. She described Charley to both men, and they also found her boot prints outside the building, where Charley had walked under a hay barn with no sides, but support posts and a roof. The rain had not washed out the tracks there.

Later, Man Killer and Chris Colt spoke over an evening campfire. At the same time, Charlotte Adams stayed in a cheap Denver boardinghouse, trying to get leads on Drago Meconi and his remaining partners. She wasn't able to and the image of Minty dying before her gun would not leave her brain. Charlotte got her traveling pack out and changed into feminine clothing. She bathed first, then put on makeup and a bonnet.

Charlotte left her room that night, her gun hidden under the folds of her clothing. She went to the depot and bought a ticket for Santa Fe. Early the next morning, Charley in a form-fitting, but conservative blue gingham dress boarded the Denver and Rio Grande train headed for New Mexico territory. She would go and get her children and move somewhere, anywhere, but she had enough of killing. The image of her shooting of Cyrus Minty just wouldn't leave her mind.

Charlotte Adams looked out the window to the rolling hills to the east. Beyond them, the high prairie ran for miles. In the distance, she saw flashes of lightning but she knew that there was no sound of thunder, for the lightning she watched was over 200 miles to the east in Kansas. The rolling hills outside Denver gave way to flatter terrain and by the time the Kansas/Colorado lines were reached it was flat in every direction. People in Colorado would make jokes while looking out toward Kansas to the east or Nebraska to the east/northeast, commenting on being able to see next Thursday or Saturday's weather.

Chris and Man Killer lay in their bedrolls and Colt was restless again. Something had been really bothering him, but he didn't know what it was.

While he lay there, he stared up at the starry sky enjoying the thick Milky Way.

With the sixth sense he always seemed to possess about these matters, Man Killer, who had seemed to be sound asleep, suddenly spoke out, "Great Scout, again this night, your heart is troubled."

Chris Colt didn't look over, he just grinned while looking up at the stars. He grinned for two reasons: one was because Man Killer always knew when something troubled him; two, because Man Killer at times like this reverted to a poetic, lyrical manner of speaking as was common among American Indians. Man Killer was the most intelligent man or boy that Colt had ever met, and he seemed to have an insatiable thirst for knowledge. Ofttimes when the two were camped in the mountains, desert, or prairie for the night, Colt would repair a saddle, tack, gun, or piece of buckskin clothing and Man Killer would fall asleep by the fire reading a new book. A millionaire by marriage, he constantly ordered new books for his extensive library.

Chris pulled out a cigar and lit it, tossing it over to Man Killer. He lit one for himself and blew the smoke skyward. Man Killer blew his in the directions of the four compass points offering blessings to the Great Mystery, who he actually believed was God, as the whites know Him. Man Killer was educated and raised essentially by Catholic missionaries who worked among the Nez Perce, but didn't really totally believe in the Word of God, or the message of Salvation until after he married the beautiful Jennifer Banta, a Christian woman herself. That, however, did not provide Man Killer with his religious beliefs. It was his own study of the Nez Perce doctrine compared with other religious teachings.

Man Killer always confounded Chris with the knowledge he had acquired that Chris didn't even know about before. Such was the time that the two men were far to the west in Grand Junction, where the Colorado River was a little more peaceful winding its way into Utah, then south into Arizona.

They had been in pursuit of two men who had held up an army payroll and had stopped in at a saloon at midday for lunch and a beer. A large sheepherder had been drinking reportedly for two days, off and on, but generally very heavily. He got into a discussion with Man Killer, which began with him referring to Man Killer as a "heathen redskin."

The shepherd, oddly enough, had been a preacher at one time, and had preached fire and brimstone from his pulpit in North Carolina, with numerous pulpit-poundings from a ham-size fist. The preacher-turned-shepherd left his congregation, wife, home, and birthplace rather abruptly after some questions about the closeness of his counseling with the wife of one of his strongest tithers. The woman reportedly had been upset with her wealthy tobacco farmer husband, and turned to the preacher for more than ministerial comfort.

Shortly, thereafter, the ex-preacher took up drink far in excess of communal practice and wandered around trying one odd job after another. Somehow, he latched on to herding sheep and was so drunk he could not remember how it started. He ended up with his own flock and was fast becoming a fine wool producer in western Colorado. His fondness for pulling a cork was also growing in proportion to his success and he could often be found in saloons celebrating whatever was in his mind at the time.

The man, whose name was ironically Ezekiel, Man Killer's childhood name, asked Man Killer if he believed in the Great Spirit, and then delivered a ten-minute lecture when Man Killer responded affirmatively.

After the man wound down a little, Man Killer countered, "You ask if I believe in the Great Spirit and I say, yes, but he is also called the Holy Ghost by you."

Ezekiel was dumbfounded momentarily, but came back with, "But you are still a red heathen and in danger of damnation."

Man Killer said, "Why is that, sir? I believe in the Holy Trinity; the Father, the Son, and the

Holy Ghost, but I call them by other names, and I
believe also in Mother Earth."

Ezekiel replied, "Y'all are a heathen Injun and
y'all cannot worship God, or our Lord and sav-
iour Jesus Christ without calling them by their
rightful names."

Man Killer said, "These are the words of
who?"

The ex-preacher said, "The Word of God. The
Bible."

Man Killer now astounded Colt, who had been
listening with an amused grin, when the Nez
Perce deputy said, "You care for sheep and I
wonder if you are familiar, sir, with the Gospel
according to John, I believe verses 10:14, 15, and
16. According to the Apostle John, Jesus said,

> *I am the good shepherd; I know my sheep and
> my sheep know me—just as the Father knows me
> and I know the Father—and I lay down my life
> for the sheep. I have other sheep that are not of
> this sheep pen.*

"By stating that He lays his life down for the
sheep, I believe Jesus makes it clear that he is
speaking of man as sheep. But that last sentence
is interesting, sir. Could he mean people like In-

dians, for example, could believe in Biblical Truth without even hearing or reading it? Could the Great Mystery be the very same as the Holy Ghost? Could the Supreme Being recognized by each Indian nation also be God? What do you think, good shepherd?"

Ezekiel said, "Ah, y'all are a durned heathen. That's what I know."

Man Killer said, "Right."

He tossed a coin on the bar and walked slowly out of the saloon with a chuckling Chris Colt following and scratching his head.

Colt blew another puff of smoke toward the sky and responded to Man Killer's remark about something being on his mind.

He said, "The man telling us about me having a sister. I guess it has been eating away at me. I wonder if I do have a sister. I remember how shocked I was when I learned I had a brother I never knew about."

Colt thought back to his first meeting with his half-brother Joshua who was half-black and half-white. Chris had, at first, had a temper tantrum and had to deal with his own racism. He sorted it out though and welcomed Joshua with open arms, making him a partner in the ranch. Since then, the two had become brothers, totally and closely.

When Chris had his tantrum, he had punched Joshua and rode off up into the mountains to think. It was a poignant story and a turning point in Chris Colt's life. He had punched Joshua and called him "nigger," a term he hated and had never used in his life. Colt, however, felt something, though, when he met the black cowboy, and the scout had learned from his red brothers to listen to his heart, because it was more honest than his head. There was something about the man's character. Colt could sense it. He was an honest, hardworking man. Chris Colt felt this strongly because he was the same way himself.

Up in the mountains later, Colt looked up at a rocky crag and saw a bald eagle fly off his cliffside aerie and wing his way eastward out over the Wet Mountain Valley. Far below him, he could see the ranch house and outbuildings of his new home. They were all like little boxes in his vision now.

He watched the eagle make lazy circles thousands of feet above the valley floor, and Colt thought back to the story he heard in the lodges of the Minniconjou, his first wife's people. Chantapeta was Lakotah and her name meant "Fire Heart." Their little girl was named Winona, which meant "First Born." She was to be the first of many, but a party of five Crow renegades cut their family life short when Colt's wife was assaulted, and she and his daughter were murdered. Colt had spent much time with her band and had heard the story of the eagle and the prairie chicken several times.

A mighty eagle flew off from her cliffside aerie, like the one Colt had just seen, and she searched for more branches to make the nest sturdier. While she was gone a gust of wind suddenly appeared over a ridgeline and blew one egg out of the large nest. Miraculously, it rolled, unhurt, all the way down the cliffside and out onto the prairie at the base of the steep mountain.

It landed squarely right in the nest of a prairie chicken. Without much ability to think and reason, the prairie hen didn't notice the extra egg, which was larger than the other five eggs all combined. She sat on the nest each day until they all hatched, and the hen started raising the young eaglet as her own. It didn't matter to the rooster and hen prairie chickens that, within a few months, one of their offspring was twice their body size. They raised their young brood as they knew how.

One day the father led his young prairie chickens single file through the sagebrush, creosote bushes, and mesquite. The eaglet was last in line, and he happened to look up into the blue sky and spot his real father, the mighty bald eagle soaring around above him in big circles.

He cried, "Oh, Father, oh, Father, look up at that mighty bird. He is so beautiful and strong and free. He is truly blessed by Wakan Tanka, the Great Spirit. What kind of bird is he, Father?"

The prairie chicken father looked at the big eagle and said, "he is an eagle, my son."

The father started to go on, but the eager young bird said, "Oh, Father, I must meditate and speak to the Great Mystery and ask him to make me like such a bird. It would be wonderful."

The father looked at his adopted son and said, "No, forget it. You can never be like him: He is an eagle, and you are just a prairie chicken."

Colt watched the big bird, far out over the valley as he swooped down toward the earth, apparently diving after a prey. Colt lost sight of him below the tops of the trees to his front. He smiled to himself and thought of the young black cowboy while he was growing up. He tried to picture in his mind's eye how many times the boy would have been told he was just a prairie chicken. He tried to picture the man as a boy, fighting and struggling to be an eagle. He would have had to. It ran in his veins, Colt thought, then grinned at himself.

He mounted War Bonnet and headed straight-away down the mountain. It was time to go home. The sun felt the same way. It didn't take Chris long at all to get down the mountain. Before long, he was at the bottom of the thick tree line and overlooking his ranch lands.

Colt saw a rider in the distance headed toward his place on the road from Westcliffe. The man was on a big dappled gray quarter horse. Colt could tell, even at a distance, that the man was the black cowboy. The scout's trained eyes were sharp and his memory had automatically filed away the cowboy's description.

The scout touched his heels to the great stallion's flanks, and they were off like the wind. The man was headed to Colt's ranch and Chris wanted to meet and talk to him. He had things to say and questions to ask. He had an apology to offer.

Just before sunset, Colt rode into the ranch yard and dismounted, leading War Bonnet into the barn. The cowboy had arrived, just minutes before, and was now speaking to Shirley, who fidgeted nervously on the front porch of the large log cabin home. Man Killer was busily moving around the area between the ranch house and barn, doing chores, and finding a place for equipment, long since dropped in various places.

Colt unsaddled, rubbed down his horse, and gave him a pail of oats and several squares of alfalfa/grass hay mix that had been stored in the barn. He petted his friend, then went to join Shirley and the black cowboy.

The black man had a serious look on his face as Chris Colt walked forward and stretched out his hand to shake. Shirley had a look of extreme relief on her face.

Colt said, "Mister, I owe you an apology for that stunt I pulled."

Colt didn't get the next word out of his mouth, because he was flying backward, and the only thing coming out of his mouth was blood from split lips. He started to stand and was met by an uppercut that sent him flying backward over the hitching rack in front of his porch. The small of his back hit the rail with a thud and Colt spun backward over it landing on his stomach and face. Shirley held her hands over her mouth and stared at the two.

Colt spit blood out of his lips and grinned at the other man, while pushing himself up with a moan. He stepped over the railing and again stuck his hand out.

Chris said, "I deserved that. I still owe you an apology for what I said and for hitting you. I don't ever say things like that."

The man said, "I know."

Colt replied, "Why are you here?"

The man said, "I've heard about you, and I brought a herd up to Beaver from Texas and was told you bought a spread here. I thought I'd finally meet my kid brother after all these years."

Shirley interrupted, "It's obvious that you two have a lot of serious talking to do, but it doesn't need to be done standing out here. Get your hands washed, both of you, and Chris tell Man Killer to do the same."

The black man said, "Man Killer, huh? Nice name. S'pose he got it for his expertise at huntin' doves?"

Colt laughed and led the way to the outside pump, hollering at Man Killer who was in the barn.

Colt said, "What's your name?"

"Joshua," he said.

"Colt?" Chris asked.

Joshua said, "No, I took the last name of Smith."

Still totally skeptical about the story he would hear, Colt said, "Why?"

Joshua looked down at his brown hand and replied, "You have to ask, Chris?"

Colt dried his hands on the towel hanging by the pumps and said, "Why are you here? What do you want from me?"

Joshua said, "Not a damned thing, Chris Colt. I just wanted to meet you, at last. We are brothers, whether you like it or not."

Colt said, "Well, this is going to be a story I need to hear."

Man Killer didn't say anything but stuck his hand out and shook with Joshua, saying, "I am Man Killer."

The man replied, "Joshua Smith."

The supper was, as usual, delicious. Mrs. Colt had prepared mashed potatoes and gravy, fried chicken, corn on the cob, and fresh bread. The meal was followed by apple dumplings and everything was washed down by several pots of hot coffee.

After dinner, Colt offered Joshua and Man

Killer cigars and they talked while they smoked and drank coffee. Shirley joined them having several cups of coffee herself.

Joshua asked, "Do you remember the Carlsons and their maid Lulubelle?"

"Sure," Chris said. "Their family was so wealthy, they were always having my father make them new shoes or boots for someone in the family. The Carlsons sometimes came back to visit, twice I think while I was growing up, but they went off when I was young."

Joshua said, "Yep, they moved back to their family plantation in Georgia. Old Man Carlson's pa died and left him a big old plantation covered with cotton and peach orchards, and plenty of slaves."

"What about them all?" Colt asked.

Joshua said, "Lulubelle was my mother. You recollect her little boy?"

Colt said, "Yeah, vaguely, a little bit older than me. That was you?"

Joshua nodded and said, "Your father was my father."

Colt stared at him and didn't know what to think or say.

Joshua went on, "He and my mother fell in love, because they lived next door to each other, and my ma used to go down to look at the falls, while he was there fishing. They talked a lot and thought the same way on most things. Many a colored women were just used by white men, but this was just different. They loved each other but nothin' could ever come of it. She was colored and a slave. He met yer ma and married her a half year later."

Colt looked up at the ceiling, then at Shirley. He finally looked at Joshua.

Colt said, "One time . . . the only time I ever saw my pa cry was a year after my ma died of consumption. I was about eleven, and I wanted to ask to go fishing with him down at the Gorge. I walked in his room, and he was holding a tintype of your ma and tears were running down his cheeks. I was really surprised, and I asked why he was crying over her picture and why did he have it. He told me that she gave it to him before, because they were friends, and he was thinking about the fun they had fishing just above Cuyahoga Falls. Then he showed me your ma's picture and said kind of matter-of-factly, 'Gee, she was awful pretty for a colored girl, wasn't she?'"

Joshua gave Colt a knowing grin.

Colt went on. "I was a boy with a boy's curiosity. I asked a question and my pa answered it. I was satisfied and never thought about that, until now."

He poured more coffee for everyone.

Finally Chris said, "You can put your horse up in the barn and bunk in the bunkhouse tonight. Man Killer'll show you. Breakfast will be just after daybreak. Shirley and I got a lot of talking to do, and I have a lot of digesting to do."

The two men left the house.

The next morning, the four ate a hearty breakfast of apple flapjacks, ham, maple syrup, and coffee, of course. A rider came up to the house before they had a chance to talk again.

A deep voice outside boomed, "Hallo the house!"

Colt hollered back, "Coffee's hot and the food's getting cold. Hurry and wash up before it's gone."

The voice laughed and yelled back, "Dadburn, you drive a hard bargain, feller. Ya talked me into it."

The sheriff was big and gruff-looking with a salt-and-pepper handlebar mustache and a twinkle in his eye. His belly hung down over his gun belt, and his six-shooter looked like it was used only once a decade or so.

He stuck out a meaty fist and said, "Sam Dearborn, local law."

Colt shook his hand and said, "Chris Colt. This is my wife, Shirley."

The sheriff smiled and tipped his dirty Stetson.

Colt continued, "And my friend Man Killer."

The sheriff looked nonplussed and offered his hand to the Indian.

The sheriff said, "Howdy, youngster."

Colt went on, "And this is Joshua."

They shook hands and the sheriff got a very strange look when Colt continued, "Joshua Colt, my brother."

"The hell you say?" Sam replied, but that was it.

He did keep staring at the two men, apparently intrigued by the resemblances, yet the very obvious differences.

The widest-eyed stare came from Joshua, though, who looked at Chris Colt with wonder and awe. With the introduction and the use of the last name of Colt when identifying Joshua, Chris had spoken volumes.

Sam wondered why he saw tears welling up in Shirley's eyes, but he figured she was a woman, and he didn't "understand them nohow." Mebbe, he figured, it was that time each month when women and mares start acting funny and crying if you so much as spit on the ground. He also couldn't understand why she was smiling at the same time she had tears in her eyes. Then she walked over and wrapped her hands around Colt's big arm and stared up at him from the side, like he had just won the Civil War all by himself, Sam observed.

The next day, Colt and Joshua rode the borders of the Colt Ranch property and talked about the place, and their backgrounds.

Walking the foothills and discussing digging ditches with little wooden gates to irrigate the pastures better, the two occasionally talked again about their background.

Finally Colt asked, "How is your ma, Joshua?"

"Dead," he replied sadly. "She passed on about two years ago, as I understand. Pox took her."

Chris said, "When did you leave home?"

Joshua said, "Civil war. Fought in an all-Negro unit, 'cept our officers were all white. After that, picking cotton and harvesting peaches would have been a bit boring, and whenever I visited Ma, I had some close calls with the Klan. They didn't really like the fact that I had been a Union soldier. I headed west, just to see what was beyond the horizon, but I kept finding a new horizon to check out."

Colt grinned and said, "You, too, huh?"

Sitting on War Bonnet and looking out over the high mountain valley, Colt pulled out two cigars, handed one to Joshua and lit both. The two men enjoyed the view and the taste of the tobacco.

Joshua went on, "I worked a riverboat for a few months on the Big Muddy, worked the docks in New Orleans, did some prizefighting, and finally signed on with a cattle outfit. Now, that was an education. A man took me in under his wing, by the name of Callihan, James C. Used to be a schoolteacher. Sat for the bar back east. He taught me how to read and speak a little. The boss, Jess Chapman, taught me about cattle. So did a lot of years of chokin' dust, meadow muffins, bad coffee, saddle sores, twisters, blisters, and stampedes."

"How long you been punchin' cows now?" Chris asked.

Joshua said, "My whole adult life. I worked two drives as a puncher, then it got around I had a way with men, so I started getting hired to ramrod drives. Been doing that for a decade about. Got two good men who always work for me, too. They're down in Canon City with my herd."

"Herd?" Colt said, "What herd?"

Joshua said, "Last year, Jim Callihan looked me up again and asked me if I wanted to go into business with him. We started picking up range cattle down in south Texas that had been running wild and were unbranded. We put them in with a bunch of longhorns we picked up off two ranches that had gone belly up and needed money bad. We would drive our gather together and split the money in half. Callihan liked the money and decided to sell to a buyer down in Trinidad. I wanted to drive them up here and see if I could get a better price from one of the wealthy mining concerns or the railroad maybe."

"How many head you got?" Chris asked.

Joshua replied, "Little over five hundred."

Colt said, "Maybe they'll fit in with our plans. I want to know if you would like to own a piece of our ranch. You will run the whole thing."

Joshua was shocked and said, "What are you talking about?"

Colt said, "Look, you and I are brothers, and we might have a lot of differences, but the same blood runs through our veins. I am a chief of scouts. That's what I do, and it will take me away for long periods of time. Number one, I need someone here I can trust, totally, all the time to watch over my wife and the ranch. Number two, I am not a cattle rancher or horse breeder. I also need someone here who knows how to run a ranch, profitably, and they have to be someone I can trust with my business. Shirley and I will buy your cattle from you at fair market value and hire you to run the ranch, or you can contribute the cattle and be one-fourth owner of the ranch. It will become what we make of it, but you will be totally in charge of the entire ranch operation."

Joshua dismounted and stared out over the ranch, holding the reins of his horse in his left and puffing on his cigar, held in his right hand.

"Totally in charge?" Joshua asked.

Chris said, "Totally."

Joshua said, "You don't owe me nothing. Why are you offering me this?"

Colt said, "You're my brother. Way life is, way people are, it's just not fair. I know I don't owe you anything, but maybe our pa did. There were certain things in this life that probably just came easier to me because of the way folks think and act. Besides that, I don't know women very well, but I can tell about a man by a few words, the way he carries himself, and the look in his eyes. Even if we weren't kin, you'd be a man I could trust to protect my wife and ranch, and I think you've probably learned a lot about the cattle and horse ranching business."

"Think so, huh?" the black cowpuncher said.

"Why'd you hit me when I offered my handshake and apology to you? You've heard stories about me, haven't you?" Chris said, puffing on his own cheroot.

Joshua said, "'Cause you had it comin'. Simple as that."

Colt replied, "That's the point. You didn't worry about stories or anything else. You did what you figured was right, period."

"So," Joshua said, "that's how a man ought to do things."

CHAPTER 6

Family Matters

A number of years had passed since that first meeting, and discovering he had an older brother was really a shock to Chris. Now he had heard that he had a sister. He wondered if it was true.

Chris heard a train whistle to the north and he jumped up, saying, "Man Killer, saddle up fast."

Man Killer jumped up and whistled like a red-tailed hawk and both horses came at a dead run. He and Colt started saddling.

Man Killer said, "Where do we go?"

Colt grinned and said, "Catch a train."

The Nez Perce asked, "Where?"

Chris said, "New Mexico."

They were soon at a siding along the tracks running parallel with the Rampart range. Man Killer quickly gathered some brush together and built a small fire right in the middle of the tracks. No sooner had the fire started blazing than the train appeared around the bend from the north. Chris rode War Bonnet out onto the tracks behind the fire and the engineer recognized him immediately, starting to slow down the steam engine on the long, slight upgrade.

Within five minutes, the two horses were loaded onto a boxcar and the men were looking for seats in one of the passenger cars. Chris looked a second time at a young lady in a bonnet and a gingham dress as he walked by, and their eyes met. He could not believe her striking beauty and there was something in her smiling eyes that just caught him. He was totally and completely in love with his wife, so that wasn't what made his eyes lock with hers. It was something else, and he didn't know what it could be.

Charley and Chris both realized simultaneously that their gazes were lasting too long, and she smiled slightly as he tipped his hat. She saw the broad sweep of his shoulders, the sinew and muscles bulging underneath his Lakotah war shirt. She observed the low-slung guns and the ruggedly handsome face, but most obvious were the smiling eyes. The man was very good-looking and desirable, but Charlotte was not attracted to him that way. She still had a deep and abiding love for James and was very loyal to his memory. There was just something about the man with the star on his chest.

Suddenly it hit Charley full force. When she first met and married James Adams, her half-brother, Chris Colt, was legendary as a cavalry chief of scouts, but after that, she learned he became a Deputy U.S. Marshal. He had since performed other legendary exploits in that capacity and James had mentioned hearing many incredible stories about him and his exploits. She had also been told about the woman who was her sister-in-law, Shirley, and how she had been kidnapped by a criminal who Chris went after and then was taken captive by a band of Cheyennes. She had heard about Colt bringing an entire herd of horses to trade for her release when the chief had asked for five ponies. She had heard that Chris and Shirley were rich, and she also heard about him taking in an unknown half-black brother named Joshua as his partner on his sprawling ranch. She had also heard much about a Texas Ranger cousin of hers named Justis Colt and about the Nez Perce Indian who became Colt's sidekick as a teenager and was now married and a millionaire. His name was Man Killer.

There were three stories Charley heard about her older brother during her time with the Apaches, though, that impressed her the most about Chris Colt, and one of them also impressed her about Man Killer very much as well. The Apaches especially respected strength and courage, even in their enemies. It was a rare commodity and very important in their culture for survival, and they did not have much respect for very many white-eyes or Mexicans. That was why they spoke so much of Chris Colt.

A story was even told of Colt leading a cavalry patrol into a hidden canyon where he discovered, and the "long-knives" attacked, a Chiricajua rancheria. Colt had gotten separated from the main unit and, wounded, was chased for miles through the rocks by many of the Apaches. During that fight, one of the warriors accidentally shot a girl from their own village who had been returning with her family from another rancheria where her two sisters had married men out of their band.

Colt had grabbed the young Apache girl and carried her many miles trying to find a good defensive position. The Apache warriors slowly crept in on his hiding place and watched as he carefully nursed the girl back to life. She had almost made the "spirit walk," but he applied poultices and bandages and healed her.

It was two days before the girl could travel and then-scout Colt had carried her in front of him on his saddle and delivered her to her village. The whole time, the white-eyes scout did not know that the warriors who had pursued him followed him back to the rancheria and watched from hiding places while he delivered her to her parents at her wickiup. He then departed and was untouched and unspoken to by any Apaches.

That story had occurred when Chris Colt was a fairly new scout for the U.S. Cavalry. The second story happened with the Chiricajua and had even impressed the great leaders Mangas Coloradas and Cochise. Again Colt was in his early twenties, when he was scouting against the Chiricajuas in southeastern Arizona. He had led another small patrol into a hidden canyon and located a rancheria, but Colt had warned the young West Point lieutenant leading the patrol that there were too many warriors in the village and they were too battle-wise for him to attack.

The young officer wanted glory, though, so in an effort to save the rest of the patrol, Colt got many of the fighters to chase him before the main attack took place, and he led the Apaches on a wild-goose chase into the Superstition Mountains, which were in Arizona.

At one point while he fled on his young buckskin gelding Nighthawk, Colt thought he had lost them for a while when he went into a deep, steep-sided cut that dropped him down over 600 feet. The warriors, as was the custom of Apache, kept sending men up on high ground, though, to keep their quarry in sight. When they saw he was going into the big cut, they went on ahead to set up an ambush from above. They also wanted to protect their rancheria hidden in a wooded and meadowed spring location in the canyon. The Apaches fired down on him from higher ground and a bullet struck a young Chiricajua girl who was walking through the canyon. The round took her through the upper thigh, and it nicked an artery running up the thick part of her leg.

Chris jumped down and bandaged her quickly, but the leg kept bleeding, the blood pumping out in spurts from the arterial cut. He knew he would get shot up, if he stayed or get captured, but he had to get the bleeding stopped. The Apaches did stop firing awhile because of the girl and they waited, some of them moving closer for better shots. Chris Colt didn't even pay attention. He grabbed his carbine and the waiting Apaches trained their sights on him and some drew back arrows. Chris, however, was single-minded now in his purpose and quickly ejected three bullets. He removed the kerchief from his neck and put the bullets inside the rolled-up kerchief. He tied them into a little stack with two bullets on the bottom and one on top, then placed the little pile directly over the girl's bullet wound. He wrapped the kerchief around the leg and tied it off tight. The bullets made an immediate direct pressure bandage that stopped the arterial bleeding almost immediately.

Colt then mounted up and fled, holding the girl, looking for a good hiding place that would also be easy to defend. His other challenge was to be near several roots and leaves he would need for a healing poultice for her wounds. He also had to cut another bullet out of her side.

Chris rode, for hours, holding the girl until his arms felt like they would fall off. He kept on until after dark and found a small seep in among some rocks, where he made cold camp. The Apache warriors had not been seen for hours, but Chris Colt knew they were always there.

Nevertheless, he sneaked back on his backtrail and did his best to obliterate his tracks.

While he nursed the girl back to health, Colt occasionally caught glimpses of the Apache warriors watching him from various hiding places, but he kept on about his business. He would nurse her back to reasonable strength and then return her to her home to recover. Two days later when he did so, he was followed by the war party, but they thought they were staying out of sight. Colt pretended as though he didn't see them, maybe just so they could save face. He assumed they respected him for what he did, but Colt was too smart to stick around and find out. After he took her to her family's wickiup and gave her to her parents, he got out of there as quickly as he thought he could without giving the appearance of being a scared jackrabbit. He always wondered if those Chiricajua braves ever knew that he was watching them, too.

The third story that Charley had heard from some of the Jicarilla Apaches who had actually been there themselves, indicated the courage of Man Killer and the leadership of Chris Colt. Several of the Jicarillas from the band she was with had been scouts for the all-black army unit called the Buffalo Soldiers, and Chris Colt had become chief of scouts for them. They were in a campaign to find and exterminate Mimbres Apache leader Victorio.

This story had been told to Charlotte after her time with them and return to white society, and her marriage to James. Charley often took food, clothing, and other gifts to the Apaches and she was told the story then, several times.

Her older brother was addressing the scouts who were also from the Mimbres, Mescalero, and Chiricajua tribes, and from the Navajo nation. His challenge was to introduce then-young Man Killer as his second-in-command and convince them to accept a Nez Perce who was also younger than most of them as one of their superiors. The way it turned out, Man Killer was quite adept at convincing them.

Chris stood tall in front of the cross-legged scouts and spoke, pausing occasionally while two translators repeated his words in Apache and Navajo. "Some of you will wonder if I will know what I am doing scouting against the Apache. I have been here before in campaigns against the Apache, the Ute, and Comanche. I wear articles from the Lakotah and Cheyenne, and even a necklace from the Nez Perce, but my heart is with all my red brothers. I know Victorio from before, and he knows me, and we have declared ourselves as enemies, but I respect him as a warrior and leader. You will all do the same. The white-eyes do not understand that you of the Apache nation can scout against your people, because our ways are different, but I understand. You who are of the great Navajo nation will not think of Victorio as a chief of an inferior tribe, for that will get your scalp on his belt. He is smart and tough and we will always respect his knowledge in warfare and his determination. We will be moving a lot through much desert, as you have all done, so you will each carry saddlebags with extra food for your horses or ponies. You will also carry extra canteens.

"I am your boss, and you will speak and hear only from me when we are on the same patrol. If any officer or NCO tries to order you or speak down to you, tell me. If you have a question, ask me.

"Some of you are spies for Victorio or Geronimo. You are here as their eyes and ears among the white-eyes. If I catch you, I will kill you. You will all keep your jobs as they are now, including those who are leaders among the scouts.

"This is Man Killer and is my second-in-command. He is young, but would be chosen chief in any of your tribes. If I die, listen to him. Now, does any man have a problem with this?"

One stocky Apache rose, a Chiricajua who knew the great Coshise as a boy. He spit on the ground.

He spoke, "I do not listen to council from a boy who has no hair between his legs even. Too-Ah-Yay-Say has spoken."

Colt said, "Okay, draw your pay from the paymaster and fork your pony. Return to your reservation."

Man Killer stood and raised his hand. All the scouts had heard about the recent knife fight he had won against a giant mountain man. They had also heard of his loyalty and courage, and most were already in awe of the young man, who seemed destined for greatness. They also admired him walking toward Too-Ah-Yay-Say with a fresh white bandage over his left shoulder. His left arm slipped out of the sling, and he tossed it aside on the ground. Colt smiled imperceptibly as he saw Too-Ah-Yay-Say's Adam's apple bob slightly with nervousness. The assistant chief of scouts walked directly up to the Apache and stuck out his hand smiling. The Southwestern scout spit down on the lad's hand.

Moving within just inches of Too-Ah-Yay-Say's

face, Man Killer reached out and yanked the man's war club from his belt. He handed it to the shocked Apache scout.

Man Killer said, "If you think I am a boy. Strike me with your war club. Strike me anywhere, as hard as you wish, just one time. Then you will hand it to me, and I will strike you one time, anywhere I want."

Chiricajua boys grew up standing at rock piles throwing stones at one another and making cuts and bruises all over their bodies, simply to learn to accept pain.

The gauntlet had been thrown down, but these two were not boys. They were both men and could kill each other with one blow, and what if his blow did not kill the Nez Perce, he thought, then he would surely make the spirit journey. He also wondered why he was now thinking of the Nez Perce as a man. Too-Ah-Yay-Say was angry at himself for he was not ready yet to make the spirit journey. He had not even taken a wife. Well, he had one briefly, but she committed adultery with his cousin and the tip of her nose was cut off for such violation of tribal law.

Sensing that the man was now having second thoughts and Man Killer had just made a true believer out of him, Colt knew that the Apache could not back down now, because he would lose face with his compatriots.

Chris said, "I am the boss and Man Killer is my second. Do you Too-Ah-Yay-Say want to argue all day like children, or do you like the money the army pays you?"

The Apache looked at Colt, sensing an "out" possibly.

Colt then gave him a big grin and said, "Maybe this is the time in each moon when Too-Ah-Yay-Say bleeds much."

All the scouts laughed heartily, especially after the translation. Too-Ah-Yay-Say started to glare at the chief of scouts but understood from all the laughter that Colt was teasing and was not really trying to humiliate him. He laughed at himself, too. In seconds, he was releasing tension with heavy laughter. Finally, he stuck out his hand and gripped forearms with Man Killer, and they shook in Indian fashion.

Man Killer was relieved, but he knew he had to impress all these men immediately after Colt's declaration about him. He was also very thankful for Chris's incredible leadership ability and quick thinking.

Charlotte Adams was also very impressed, as she could really tell what her brother was made of from those three stories. The other thing that impressed her was the story she had heard about her other brother, the black one, Joshua. She heard about how he and a white woman had fallen deeply in love, and he had dived in front of her during a gun attack by Ku Klux Klan members. He had been shot numerous times shielding her with his body while shooting back himself. Joshua had lingered near death for weeks but survived, but the woman left forever to keep him from ever getting shot again.

Charlotte thought about that, and how much she missed James and a tear formed in one eye while she looked out the window of the train. She thought about the other story she had heard about her unknown family, and it was her favorite of all. It was the story of the courage of Shirley Colt herself.

Chris Colt, Man Killer, and Colt's attorney Brandon Rudd had been held hostage in a town that had been constructed for and by outlaws, as safe haven for outlaws to hide out and spend money in. Chris Colt was even tortured and bravely watched and joked while his little finger was sawed off with a knife. Shirley Colt and two other women, armed to the teeth, went in to the town and rescued their men, having a vicious shootout with killers in the process.

Charley thought about approaching her brother and her heart was still pounding thinking about him being seated a short distance behind her on the train. All these years now, she knew Chris Colt was her brother, and she kept hearing incredible stories about him. She knew he was wealthy, but she did not want him to think she was approaching him because she wanted money. Her pride would not allow it. She was also afraid that he would reject her if she did tell him the truth.

Charlotte was in a dilemma. She desperately wanted to meet her brother, speak with him, hug him, but she felt that the time wasn't right. She would first work her way out of debt. She would get her daughters back and buy a new home, maybe in Colorado. Then she would go and present herself to her two brothers, and meet her sister-in-law who she was already so impressed with. But still, Charley wanted desperately to speak with Chris anyway.

Finally, she made a bold move. Charlotte got out of her seat and moved back to the seat where Chris was. Man Killer had taken the empty bench seat behind Colt, so they each could stretch out and sleep during the journey.

She stood above Chris and said, "Marshal, excuse me, but may I sit with you momentarily?"

Chris stood up and removed his hat, smiling, "Of course, ma'am, please sit down."

She sat and Chris Colt again could not believe the breathtaking beauty of the woman. He still was interested only in his wife, but he certainly could appreciate beauty in other women, and this one was a knockout.

He said, "Is there something I can help you with, ma'am?"

She said, "Yes, sir. I am headed to Santa Fe and wondered how far it is. Do you happen to know?"

Chris said, "Well, as a matter of fact, I do, ma'am. In fact, we're headed there ourselves. From where we are right now, ma'am, it's about 350 miles. We should arrive sometime tomorrow."

Charlotte said, "Can you imagine that? Travel nowadays has gotten so rapid."

Chris said, "I believe that someday trains will be able to travel a distance like that in just a few hours."

Charley said, "You don't mean that, sir? How could a train ever go that fast?"

Colt said, "Maybe they could build a bigger locomotive or something. I don't rightly know, but I believe it will happen someday. You know they have a thing called the parachute now. You can jump off very tall cliffs and sail down to the ground like a thistle with it. It is like a giant umbrella."

"You don't mean it?" she said. "I just cannot hardly fathom it."

Colt said, "I'm sure you've heard of Thomas Edison and the incandescent lightbulb?"

She said, "Yes, I have. Mr. Edison is truly amazing and some of his inventions."

Colt went on, "But have you heard of Alexander Graham Bell and his invention where you can speak into an instrument kind of like a telegraph, but you can actually speak and hear the other person?"

"Sir, you don't mean it?" she exclaimed.

Then she went on resignedly. "Society is just getting so modern. I have even heard people speak of having buggies someday without horses to pull them."

Chris said, "Makes perfect sense to me. If we can ride in a train like this with a locomotive pulling it with no horses, I can see them making something like this only smaller someday."

Chris thought back to his first long train ride down toward Santa Fe, and how it was a bit different from this one in the comfortable car. He and Man Killer had been summoned to help a military unit at Fort Union some hours northeast of Santa Fe.

It was dark out and shortly before dawn when Chris Colt and Man Killer rode out the end of the northwest gate of the Coyote Run Ranch. They had only to ride downhill on the Cotopaxi Trail for five miles, and they would be at the Arkansas River and the tracks running down to Canon City. A freight train came by around daylight, which they were able to board in a boxcar and ride on to through Canon City to Pueblo. From there, they transferred to another freight train that ran south to New Mexico.

North of Las Vegas, they unloaded near Fort Union, and made the short ride into the fort on the remnants of the now dwindling Santa Fe Trail. With the introduction of the railroads all over the West, many trails like the Santa Fe had dwindled down to a small trickle of traffic. Prior to that, the Santa Fe Trail, which came down through old Bent's Fort and went south along the

Front Range into New Mexico Territory, was a mile wide with many deep wagon ruts in it. Fort Union had been the major quartermaster depot for the entire Southwest and freighter wagons arrived and departed several times a day, 365 days per year. Besides that, numerous wagon trains used the trail to flood into the Wild West frontier.

The rapid building of railroads all over the United States and now especially in the West was really killing wagon and freighter traffic. The only thing that had saved James Adams was the different angle of carrying and protecting valuable keepsakes and expensive items. Along with that had been the chance to carry occasional secret government payrolls. The rails had been the biggest purchaser of steel and Colt and Charley got a shock when this was brought up.

Eyes closed in the seat behind the siblings, Man Killer softly said, "You will soon learn that the most important invention now, is processed steel."

Charley and Chris said simultaneously, "Huh?"

Man Killer still didn't open his eyes. Charlotte stared at the handsome Indian, who she figured to be around her age.

She said, "How would you know that? You look like, a—"

Man Killer interrupted, "A dumb Indian?"

Charley was offended and made no secret of hiding it, saying, "Why you impudent ass! I had no intention of saying any such thing. I am not a racist, especially toward the American Indian. Nor am I ignorant. I was going to say that you looked too young to be so versed in such business matters."

He sat straight up and listened to her reprimand, an impassive look on his face.

When she finished, he replied, "Ma'am, I did not mean to insult you, and I apologize. I am aware of the facts because my wife and I own three of the forty-some steel foundries that exist in Pittsburgh, Pennsylvania."

Charlotte said, "That is outstanding, sir, but I hope you don't think that I am shocked. I know you are the famous Man Killer, and this gentleman is the equally famous Chris Colt."

Chris nodded and smiled at her. She knew who they were but they didn't know who she was. But he wouldn't ask. In the West, it was never polite to ask a person's name or background. One was always supposed to wait until it was offered. There were too many former Civil

War generals serving as cavalry troopers, out-
laws-turned-lawmen, and lawmen-turned-out-
laws. There were barons who had become
cowboys, and lawyers who had become trail
cooks. Many came to the West to start a new life,
so backgrounds were not inquired about in most
circles.

Charlotte did volunteer, "I have been foolish, I
believe. I've been off trying to find the killers of
my husband. I'm afraid I wanted vengeance
without thinking about how to obtain it once
they were located."

Colt said, "I'm sorry, but why didn't you let
the law handle it, ma'am?"

She said, "They didn't handle anything; besides I thought that I could at least bring some
end to it if I pursued the scoundrels myself and
saw them brought to justice. I still believe that is
true, but I maybe don't have the heart for it."

Colt understood. He thought back to the time
that he hunted down the Crow war party who
murdered his first wife and daughter. He did feel
an ending after sending each to the "happy hunting ground" as white men called it.

Colt remembered his meeting with Chief
Joseph when he delivered Man Killer, then
Ezekiel, and the horse herd. Chris was under or-

ders to report to O.O. Howard, but he had learned that Shirley, who was then his fiancée, had been captured by either Sioux or Cheyenne and was being held captive. He had sent word to his blood-brother Crazy Horse to locate her among the many bands traveling around and trying to avoid the "bluecoats" since the death of Long Hair Custer on the banks of the Greasy Grass. Colt was on the horns of a dilemma. He wanted to go after her, but didn't know what he should do.

He thought back to the first cigar he shared with the wise Chief Joseph when they first met. Hearing through the grapevine that Colt had been blinded by a grizzly bear attack and was helpless in Idaho, she had sold her successful restaurant and adjoining house in Bismarck, North Dakota Territory, left it all behind and traveled west to find and stand by Colt. On the way, she had been captured by a small band of Cheyenne. Finally hearing this, Colt had sent word to Crazy Horse to find her. This was on his mind constantly when he was sent to the village of Joseph by General O.O. "One-Armed" Howard. He was to befriend the chief and convince him to move to the Fort Lapwai reservation. Colt first spent the night there, requesting council with the notable leader.

The next morning was a memorable one for Colt as he got a full measure and insight into the man called Chief Joseph. He was a leader and an orator. It was no wonder that the perceptive "Christian General" wanted Colt to court the man. Other chiefs would certainly seek this man's council.

First, the wise old Nez Perce leader surmised and told Chris Colt exactly why he was there. He explained that Colt had been ordered by General Howard to come and meet with him, win favor with him, and convince him to do as the general wanted.

After that, amazed by the chief's simple, yet profound wisdom, Colt sought his council on another matter. He wanted to know what to do about Shirley. It was time to speak about her and find out what Joseph thought he should do.

Colt said, "Chief Joseph, I have a woman who makes my heart beat hard and steals my sleep from me many nights."

Joseph grinned.

Colt continued, "She has been taken captive by a band of the Chyela or the Lakotah, but I do not know where to find her or what to do."

Joseph poured himself another cup of coffee, sweetened it, and started drinking. He kept sipping the coffee and enjoying his cigar, and it was as if he had not heard a word Colt said. Chris knew to keep his mouth shut, as the intelligent leader was giving Colt's problem serious thought.

After ten minutes, Joseph said, "You have worked with the cavalry. You felt you had to bring Ezekiel and our ponies to us. You have worry that the horse soldiers may start war with the Nez Perce. You think of all these things that weigh heavy on your heart, but your heart is also sad, because the woman you dream of each night is somewhere. She is captive and your mind sees the many things you do not want for her. Should you just ride toward the lands of the Lakotah, or should you do your work for the cavalry first?"

Colt grinned and took a sip of coffee.

Chief Joseph said, "Where were you born?"

Colt said, "Back east, in a place called Ohio."

"I learned about it at mission school," the chief replied.

"If my wife was taken from me by your people, and they hid her somewhere in Ohio," Joseph said, "would I go to Ohio and find where she has been hidden?"

Colt said, "No. It would be impossible for you to do."

Chief Joseph said, "But does not Ohio have trees and rocks and dirt and clouds like here?"

Colt said, "It doesn't look like this land but it has all those things."

Joseph went on, "I grew up hunting and fighting and fishing as a Nez Perce. I have fought the bear and taken many scalps. I have counted coups. Am I not a good tracker, do you think, Colt?"

Chris said, "Of course. You would have to be a good tracker. You wouldn't have become chief."

"Then," Joseph said, "could I not go to Ohio and look for a sign and find my wife?"

Colt said, "No, it would still be impossible."

Joseph said, "Then who would I ask to go find her for me?"

Colt said, "You could ask me. I am white. I am from Ohio. It would be pretty easy for me to find a Nez Perce woman there."

Joseph poured another cup of coffee and spent another two minutes drinking it and enjoying the taste.

Finally, he spoke, "Wasn't she taken by someone who was Sioux or Cheyenne?"

Chris said, "Yes."

Joseph said, "Are not the Sioux brother to the Cheyenne?"

Colt said, "Yes."

"Are you not brother to Crazy Horse, who is Oglala Sioux?"

"Yes, I have sent word for him to find her."

Joseph said, "Then you have done the right thing. Crazy Horse will look because he is your brother. He will find her because he is Sioux, and the Sioux and Cheyenne are like the left hand and the right hand. You must now do your work and trust to your brother."

There it was, pure, simple, the answer to Colt's problem. It was brilliant because it was so simple, as is the way with most good answers. Again using very simple logic, the mighty chief showed Chris Colt that he basically could do nothing that many miles away and should trust to his blood-brother Crazy Horse to see to her safety.

After that, trying hard to do the work he was hired to do but finding his sympathies and common sense was instead with Joseph and the plight of the Nez Perce people, Chris Colt joined them in their flight for freedom.

His first child, a son, had been named Joseph

after the famous leader, and Chris communicated to Joseph whenever he could.

Colt looked over at the woman who was really his sister and said, "Ma'am, would it offend you if I smoke a cigar?"

Charley said, "Absolutely not, Marshal Colt, I love the smell of a man smoking a pipe or cigar."

Colt lit up a cigar and blew the smoke toward the ceiling.

He thought for a minute, then said, "Ma'am, I can certainly understand your wanting to pursue the men who killed your husband, but have you really considered letting the law take care of it?"

She didn't answer but sort of nodded.

Chris went on, "Let's say that you had a little boy, and he was very sick. Let's say you were worried that he might die. Now, I know you would want to do anything you could to make him better. Right? So what would you do?"

Charley thought of her beautiful little daughters and said, "Why, I'd summon the doctor, of course."

Colt smiled and said softly, "Oh."

She looked at him and the weight of his simple two-letter word hit her hard.

Charley said, "Let the experts do the work?"

Colt smiled and blew smoke at the ceiling.

Chris told her about his meeting with Chief Joseph, and she thought to herself, Joseph told him to trust his brother Crazy Horse to do the job for him. Why couldn't she tell her own brother right here in front of her to do the work for her? She just could not make herself say anything. The time was not right. Charley needed to think. She excused herself and started for the back door of the car. Colt jumped up and grabbed a pitcher of water to put out a hot spark that landed on a piece of paper that had been left on a seat by a peddler who had moved to the back of the car. Charlotte got a few breaths of air and returned to the seat, adjusting her bonnet after she sat down.

Man Killer had been doing a lot of thinking while lying on the seat pretending to be asleep. Chris Colt taught him to be a tracker, and he was working out a trail.

Charlotte said, "I suppose I should not worry about this problem and just turn it over to the law. I am just a woman. What can I do?"

Chris started to respond, but didn't know that Man Killer was thinking about a story told him by Colt's cousin, Texas Ranger Justis Colt. He was told the story by his Comanche wife and had repeated the tale to Man Killer.

The Nez Perce said, "May I speak to you of some bears?"

Oh no, Chris humorously thought, here goes Chief Joseph Junior again.

Charley was puzzled but she said, "Please?"

Man Killer said, "There was a grizzly bear cub whose mother was very very large. They lived on the edge of the high plains and sometimes went into the baby hills that played at the feet of the big mountains. The little bear loved his mother very much and stayed close to her. As he grew, he would travel farther away from her to learn about the mountains and the prairie and the other animals that lived there. First, when he saw the other animals, he wanted to play with them, but as he got bigger and older, he wanted to eat them.

"The little bear liked to eat very much, and he really liked to eat the mountain blueberries, which grew on the side of one of the biggest mountains.

"The place where the berries grew was on the side of the mountain in a steep gulch. The berry patch was up above a spring that came down from the rocks and began a small stream that ran down the mountain and told green grasses and pretty flowers to grow there. The hummingbirds used to come and drink much from the flowers and the other animals from the mountains liked to eat the long green grass that grew on the slope.

"One day, the mama bear was sleeping with the little one, while Father Sun was making his walk across the top of the sky. They were very tired from digging marmots out of a hillside.

"The baby bear woke up and wanted some berries, so he walked on a game trail that ran along the mountain where it was very deep and steep. If you pushed a rock off the side of the trail, and it fell over the cliff, you could sing many words in a lullaby before you could hear the rock hit the bottom.

"Every time before, when the mama took him to eat berries they would walk down the ridge to the stream, then walk up the stream to the berry patch, but the baby bear was young and small and could easily walk on the trail, so he went straightaway across the face of the mountain like the deer and the sheep with the big horns did.

"When the mama woke up, she looked around and smelled but she could not hear, or smell, or see her little one. She smelled his scent on the trail, and she followed along, because she was worried and did not want him to get eaten by the big cat. When she came to the small trail, she walked very carefully so she would not drop off the side, but she was a grizzly bear and was very big. She came to one spot where the cliff came out over the trail, and she could not fit by without falling over the edge, but she was a good mother and her baby was farther on. She moved very slowly and carefully and tried to move past the rocks, but she lost her balance and fell far below to her death.

"The next day, the baby found her body and cried for a long time. He went and drank from the stream and then lay down next to his mama and fell asleep.

"When he woke up, another bear was sniffing him, a big bear, and he was very scared. He looked around, and he saw that it was a mother bear, too, because there was another bear that was a boy, but he was bigger than the orphan bear."

Charley Colt had heard such manner of speech among the Apache and had used it herself. She was entranced by Man Killer's story.

He went on, "The little orphan bear was very frightened but the big bear said, 'Do not be scared, little bear. I will eat your mama, because I am a bear, but you can be my son.'

"He did not want to see her eat his mother, so he walked into the trees and bawled, but he was happy to have a new mama. He also had a new brother.

"The big boy bear and the mama were black bear's, but the orphan was a grizzly bear, and you know they grow to be very, very big, with very long claws and long teeth?"

Charley nodded affirmatively as Man Killer continued, "The orphan bear looked at his new brother and was very proud of his new family. His new brother was very strong and very brave and would scare away many animals, and the orphan bear wished he could do the same as his big brother. The big brother liked showing off for his orphan brother because it made him feel even stronger and braver than he was.

"This kept happening and the big brother became a mighty bear. Do you know why? One reason was because the orphan bear watching him made him become braver and stronger and soon that was all he knew.

"The little bear was a grizzly bear, so he kept growing and getting bigger and stronger and braver. Soon, he was as big as the big brother bear, but he did not know it, because to him the other bear was always his big brother and his hero."

"What was the orphan bear to the big brother bear and the mother bear?" Charlotte asked.

Man Killer said, "They both saw the orphan grow into a mighty grizzly that could maybe kill them and eat them if it wanted to, but to him they were still his big brother bear and his mama bear.

"One day, the three of them were walking along a big ridgeline looking for a honey tree. They went around a bend in the trail and there was a big red silvertip grizzly bear.

"He stood up on his hind legs and said, 'I will kill you and eat you first, big bear. Then I will kill and eat the others.'"

Charley very absorbed now, said, "What happened?"

"Both brothers stood on their hindlegs and the older brother started forward, but the red grizzly raised his paw and said, 'No, I said I will kill the big bear first,' and he pointed at the orphan bear.

"The orphan bear was very shocked and he said, 'Me? I will fight you, but my brother is the big bear.'

"The big red grizzly started laughing, and he laughed so hard that he could not stop, and the orphan bear was able to jump on him and kill him. Then he looked up at the sky and Father Sun and gave out a mighty roar. His big brother and mother ran to him and laughed and hugged him.

"The orphan bear said, 'Why did he laugh and point at me?'

"The mother bear said, 'Because you are the big bear, not your brother.'

"The orphan bear said, 'But he is my big brother.'

"The mother bear smiled at him and said, 'Not anymore. Now he is just your brother, for you are both big strong bears.'

"Then the three bears walked away looking for a honey tree where they could eat and be happy. Great Scout, can I have one of those cigars?"

Colt chuckled and handed his compadre a small cigar. Charlotte had a tear in the corner of one eye.

Chris said, "Ma'am, could you make sense of that story?"

Quietly, Charley said, "Yes."

Chris looked at Man Killer who just clamped down on his cigar and puffed smoke. Charlotte pulled out a hanky and dabbed at her eyes. She returned to her seat, leaving Chris Colt wondering what was happening.

Charley wondered how Man Killer could have guessed she was Colt's sister. How could he possibly have known, or was it just an incredible coincidence?

The three rode on in relative silence and soon the train slowed to take on water and firewood near Colorado City. A northbound freight train was also stopped and taking water at the same time. Still bothered by Man Killer's story, she was looking out the window and saw Ezekiel Park, the black conspirator in her husband's death.

All thoughts of returning to Santa Fe left her head, for Charlotte was now seeing another responsible in the death of her husband.

She waved at Chris and Man Killer and said, "I think I'll get off here. Nice talking to you gentlemen."

Charley rushed from the train and looked for somewhere to change clothes. There was an outbuilding behind the depot. It was not really what she wanted but would have to do for now.

Charlotte quickly undressed and bound her ample bosom tightly, then put on her male clothes. She dabbed the bottom of the dress she removed into a bucket of water from a nearby well. Then she used that to wash off the makeup she wore. Charlotte rubbed some dirt on her face and felt like she was ready to go. She checked the loads in her gun, spun it backward into her holster, took a deep breath, and grabbed her bag in hand, heading for the back of the train. She looked for freight cars with open doors to climb into. Charlotte found one about five cars back and she looked around for the brakeman or anybody looking for train hoppers. Seeing none, she climbed up into the car and waited for the train to pull out again.